A Few Hours of Sunlight

BY FRANÇOISE SAGAN

A Few Hours of Sunlight

Translated from the French by Terence Kilmartin

HARPER & ROW, PUBLISHERS

New York, Evanston,

San Francisco, London

TO MY SISTER

Inconnue, elle était ma forme préférée,
Celle qui m'enlevait le souci d'être un homme,
Et je la vois et je la perds et je subis
Ma douleur, comme un peu de soleil dans l'eau froide.

—PAUL ELUARD

PART ONE

Paris

1

Lately it had been happening to him practically every
morning. Unless he had gotten so seriously drunk the night
before that the chore of getting up, taking a shower, dressing,
became so weightless, so unconscious almost, that he did it
blindly, rapt, or rather rescued from himself by his fatigue.
But the other days were more frequent and more painful: he
would wake up at dawn, his heart pounding with fear—
with what, by now, he could only call his fear of life—and
wait for the endless recapitulation to begin inside his head:
his anxieties, his failures, and the grim calvary of the day
ahead. His heart still pounding, he would try to go back to
sleep, to forget about himself. Hopeless. He would sit up in
bed, reach for the water bottle beside him, swallow a tepid
mouthful, as stale and flat as his life these past three months,
and he would think "What's the matter with me? What's
the matter with me?" with a mixture of wretchedness and

rage, for he was a proud man, and the possibility of a nervous breakdown, however familiar in the lives of people he genuinely respected, was as humiliating as a slap in the face. He had never thought much about himself since growing up; living his life had sufficed; and to be suddenly confronted with this sickly, wan, overwrought creature filled him with superstitious terror. Could it really be he, this man of thirty-five, trembling for no reason on the edge of a bed in the hours before daybreak? Was it to this that thirty years of laughter, light-heartedness, and love's occasional grief had brought him? He sank back on the pillow, hugging it to his cheek as though by its very nature it might be the source of blessed sleep. But his eyes remained open. He felt cold and pulled up the blankets, and he was too hot and threw them off again, and he could not stem the inward shivering, desperation, absolute misery.

Of course, he ought to have turned to Eloise and made love to her. But he couldn't. It had been three months since he touched her, three months since they had even talked about it. . . . Almost as though she could sense something sickly, something strange in him, as though she was sorry for him. And the idea of her pity tormented him, far more than her anger or her possible infidelity. He would have given anything to want her, to fling himself upon her, into the warmth of another body, violently, forget himself in something other than sleep. But he couldn't. And the few timid overtures which she herself had dared had incredibly disgusted him. He who had so loved making love that he had been able to in the most ludicrous or the most bizarre circumstances, indiscriminately, found himself impotent, lying in bed beside a beautiful woman who attracted him, and of whom he was, moreover, extremely fond.

No, he was exaggerating. They had made love, once, three weeks ago, after that famous party of Jean's. But he couldn't remember it. He had drunk too much that evening—with good reason—and he recalled only a confused, blind tussle in the double bed and the relief, on waking, of having scored a point. As though the brief moment of pleasure given and received had somehow made up for the nights of anxiety, feeble excuses, and feigned nonchalance. Hardly a triumph. Life, which up to now had given him everything, or so he thought—and it was one of the reasons for his success—life was receding from him as the sea abruptly withdraws, abandoning a rock it has caressed too long. The notion of himself as an ancient rock made him smile for a moment, a bitter little smile. But he felt life was in truth draining away from him, as though from some secret wound. Time was no longer simply passing; it was vanishing. And however much he counted his blessings— good health, an interesting job, all-round success—it all seemed as pointless and boring as the Litany of the Blessed Virgin. Dead . . . the words were dead.

The evening at Jean's had also added a repulsive physiological aspect to the whole thing: he had left the drawing room for a moment to comb his hair and wash his hands. The soap had slipped and fallen to the floor under the washbasin, and he had bent down to pick it up. It was lying under a pipe, as though hiding there; it was pink and suddenly it seemed to him obscene. He had put out his hand to pick it up, and couldn't, as if some sly nocturnal animal lurked in the shadows awaiting the touch of his hand, and he was suddenly frozen with horror. He had stood up, sweating, and stared at himself in the mirror, with a sort of objective curiosity, sprung from the core of his intelligence, which quickly gave way to terror. Taking a deep breath like a diver, he had crouched down once more and picked up the soap. But he had instantly flung it into the basin, as, on a country walk, one flings away a sleeping snake mistaken for a stick, and he had spent several minutes bathing his face in cold water. It was then that he thought it was "more than just liver trouble, or tiredness, or the times we live in." It was then that he admitted that "it" really existed and that he was ill.

But what was there to do? Who is more alone than the man who has chosen his path of gaiety, happiness, amiable cynicism—chosen it naturally, instinctively—and who loses them all at one stroke, in Paris, in the year of grace 1967? The idea of a psychiatrist humiliated him; indeed he profoundly rejected it, from a spiritual pride which he was half inclined to regard as his best quality. So he had no alternative but to carry on in silence. Or try to carry on. Besides, the blind faith he had always had in life and its chances led him to look on the whole thing as temporary. Time, the only authority he recognized, had dissolved his loves, joys, sorrows, sometimes his ideas; there was no reason why it shouldn't dissolve "this thing," too. The trouble was that "this thing" was amorphous, indefinable, he had no idea what it was. And time, perhaps, is powerless against the unknown.

2

He had spent the whole morning at his newspaper, where he worked on the foreign desk. The world was full of violent and absurd happenings, to which his colleagues reacted with smug indignation that exasperated him. Three months ago, he would have happily joined in their outraged clamor, but he no longer could. He even felt slightly annoyed at the way people in the Middle East, the United States, or elsewhere kept trying to distract him from his real problem: himself. With the world on the brink of chaos, who had the inclination, or the time, to worry about his petty troubles? And yet, what about all the hours he himself had spent listening to tales of despair and confessions of failure, what about all the bogus rescue operations he had performed? But no; people were milling around him, eyes bright with excitement, and he was alone, suddenly as bereft of beliefs as a stray dog, as self-absorbed as a senile old man, and as useless.

Abruptly he decided to go and talk to Jean on the floor above. Jean was the only person he could think of at the moment who was sufficiently detached and at the same time sufficiently sensitive to intimations of unhappiness.

At thirty-five, Gilles was still handsome. "Still," because at twenty he had been extraordinary looking, with a splendor of which he had never been consciously aware but which he had, nevertheless, jubilantly made use of, and which had long attracted women and men indiscriminately—the latter in vain. Fifteen years later, he was thinner, more masculine, but there remained in his walk, in his movements, something of the radiant youth he had once been. Jean, who had been madly in love with him in those days, though without telling him or indeed admitting it to himself, felt a pang as he saw him come in. The leanness, the blue eyes, the mop of black hair, the tenseness . . . As a matter of fact, he had been getting more and more tense of late—Jean should do something about him. But he couldn't get around to it: Gilles had for so long represented in his eyes the embodiment of carefree happiness that he hesitated to speak to him as one hesitates to attack a cherished image. Supposing the image were to crumble; supposing he, Jean, who had never been anything but fat, bald, and ravaged by life, were to discover that there was no such thing as a congenitally happy man? It would not be the first illusion he had lost, but it seemed to him, in its very naïveté, one of the most painful to lose. He pushed a chair towards Gilles, who sat down cautiously—for the room was literally overflowing with files strewn over the desks, the floor, and the mantelpiece—and accepted Jean's proffered cigarette. The window gave onto a view of gray and blue rooftops, a world of gutters and television aerials that had always enchanted Gilles. Today he ignored it.

8

"Well," said Jean, "nice, isn't it?"

"The assassination, you mean? Yes, it's pretty awful, I must say." He sat silent, his eyes downcast.

A minute went by, and Jean put away some files, whistling as though a minute's silence between them was the most natural thing in the world. It was his last try; he resigned himself; a wave of tenderness swept over him as he remembered Gilles's warmth and kindness and solicitude when his own wife had left him, and he suddenly felt appallingly selfish. For two whole months he had sensed that Gilles was unhappy, for two whole months he had avoided speaking to him about it. It was much too long for a friend. Nevertheless, since Gilles was allowing him, or rather forcing him, to take the initiative, he could not resist some mild histrionics. Everyone is like that after thirty: any important event, public or private, virtually requires some dramatic touches if one is to make the most of it or really be affected by it. So Jean stubbed out his half-smoked cigarette in the ashtray, sat himself down, and folded his hands. He looked Gilles in the eye for a moment, coughed, and said soberly:

"Well?"

"Well what?" said Gilles. Now that it came to the point, he wanted to leave, but at the same time knew that he would not leave, that he had forced Jean to this cross-examination. Worse, he already felt a certain relief.

"Well, there's something wrong, isn't there?"

"Yes."

"And there has been for a month or two, right?"

"Three."

Jean had picked the period at random in order to show Gilles that he had been keeping an eye on him and had refrained from speaking to him earlier only out of diffidence. But Gilles thought at once: "The bastard's trying to show

9

how shrewd and perspicacious he is, and he's a whole month wrong." He went on:

"Yes, for the past three months . . . my life's been going badly."

"Any precise reasons?" asked Jean, lighting another cigarette briskly. For a moment Gilles hated him; why couldn't he drop the police-chief act, the tone of the dispassionate expert; why couldn't he cut the comedy? At the same time, he simply had to talk; a warm, smooth, irresistible current was carrying him toward the confessional.

"None."

"That's more serious," said Jean.

"It might be and it might not," said Gilles.

The antagonism in his voice roused Jean from his psychiatrist's role. He got up, walked round the table, and put his hands on Gilles's shoulder, murmuring: "Poor old Gilles, don't worry," which, horror of horrors, brought tears to Gilles's eyes. He really must be at the end of his tether. He stretched out his hand, picked up a ball-point pen from the desk, and began clicking the point in and out with intense concentration.

"What's up?" asked Jean. "Are you sure you're not ill?"

"It's nothing. There's nothing wrong with me. I've lost interest in everything, that's all. It's a fashionable disease, isn't it?"

He gave a brief, sardonic laugh. In fact, the thought that it might be as common as all that, more or less officially recognized by doctors of every type, was no comfort to him. On the contrary, it irritated him. If nothing else, he ought at least to be able to think of himself as a special case.

"The fact is," he went on with an effort, "I don't want to work, I don't want sex, I don't want to move. All I want to do is spend the day alone in bed, with the sheets over my head."

"Have you tried it?"

"Of course. Not for long, though. By nine in the evening I was suicidal. My bed seemed dirty, I couldn't stand the smell of my own body, and I detested the cigarettes I usually smoke. Do you find that normal?"

Jean groaned, more shocked by these particulars of mental distress than he would have been by the details of some obscenity. He made a last attempt at a logical explanation.

"What about Eloise?"

"Eloise? She puts up with me. We never had much to say to each other, as you know. She's very fond of me. On top of it all, I'm impotent. Not only with her, but in general. At least, almost. Anyway, even if I *can* manage it, it bores me. So . . ."

"That's nothing serious," said Jean. "It'll soon pass."

He tried to laugh it off, reduce it to another story of a young rooster whose pride has been ruffled.

"You ought to see a good doctor, take some vitamins, get some fresh air, and you'll be chasing the girls again in a fortnight."

Gilles looked up. He was beside himself.

"Don't keep harping on that! I couldn't care less about it, don't you understand. I don't want anything, don't you see—it's not just women. I don't want to exist. Do you know any vitamins for that?"

There was a silence.

"How about a Scotch?" said Jean.

He opened a drawer, took out a bottle, and offered it to Gilles, who swallowed a mouthful mechanically. He shuddered, and shook his head.

11

"That doesn't help any more, either. Except to make me sleep; or put me into a stupor. Drink's no fun any longer. And in any case, it wouldn't be a real solution, would it?"

Now it was Jean's turn to take a long gulp from the bottle.

"Come on," he said, "let's go for a stroll."

They went out. Paris was ravishing in the poignant blue haze of early spring. And the streets were still the same, with the same bistros: the Sloop, where they all used to go drink at times of crisis, and the bar where Gilles used to go and telephone Maria on the sly, in the days when he was in love with her. Oh God, how he remembered those days, trembling with anxiety in the overheated booth, reading and rereading the graffiti on the walls without taking them in, while her number rang and rang and did not answer. How he used to suffer, feigning unconcern in front of the *patronne* as he ordered a drink afterward, downing it in one gulp, inwardly convulsed with rage and misery; but at least he had been alive! And that agonizing period when his life had been subject to someone else's whim, when he had been trampled on, seemed almost enviable compared to the present. He had been hurt, but that wound at least had had a name.

"How about going away?" said Jean. "We could fix up an assignment somewhere or other for a couple of weeks."

"I couldn't face it," said Gilles. "The idea of strange hotels, catching planes, seeing people . . . I couldn't do it. And packing and unpacking . . . no thanks."

Jean glanced at him out of the corner of his eye, wondering for a moment if he was not putting it on. Gilles had always enjoyed fooling around, especially if one played up to him. But now he wore an expression of fear and disgust that Jean found utterly convincing.

"What if we spent an evening together with a couple of girls, as we used to in the old days? Pretend we're a pair of country bumpkins on the loose? No, that's silly. . . . What about your book on America?"

"There have been fifty better ones already. And how do you think I could write anything remotely interesting when I've lost all interest in everything myself?"

The mention of the book was the last straw. It was true that he had wanted to write a book about America, which he knew well; true that he had thought about it and even done an outline. And it was also true that he would be incapable at present of writing a single line or developing a single idea on the subject. What on earth had happened to him? What was he being punished for, and by whom? He had always got along well with his friends and been rather tender with women. He had never deliberately done anyone any harm. Why, at the age of thirty-five, had life recoiled in his face, like a poisoned boomerang?

"I'll tell you what's the matter with you," said Jean's voice in his ear, a soothing, unbearable voice, "you're overtired, you're . . ."

"You can't tell me that's the matter with me," Gilles suddenly yelled in the middle of the street, "you can't tell me because you don't know! Because even *I* don't know! And what's more," he added with consummate unfairness, "I wish to God you'd leave me alone!"

People were staring at them, and he reddened suddenly, put out his hand to take Jean by the lapel as though to say something more, then turned on his heel and without another word walked swiftly away in the direction of the river.

3

Eloise was waiting for him; Eloise was always waiting for him. She was a model in a fashion house—a not particularly successful one—and she had enthusiastically installed herself in his apartment one evening two years before, when he had been so tortured by the memory of Maria that he could bear his loneliness no longer. Blonde, brunette, or redhead according to the seasons, for photogenic reasons which he had given up trying to understand, she had beautiful blue eyes, a good body, and unfailing good humor. For a long time they had gotten along very well on a certain level, but now he wondered desperately what to say to her, how to get through the evening with her. He could always pretend that he had to go out to dinner and leave her behind—she wouldn't take offense—but he shrank from facing the outside world once more: Paris, the streets, the night. He wanted to hide somewhere and be alone.

He had a three-room flat in the rue Monsieur le Prince, which he had never finished decorating. At first, he had enthusiastically put up shelves, installed stereo equipment, bookcases, television—in a word, all the gadgets which are supposed to add to the pleasure and enrichment of life. Now these possessions bored him; although he used to read voraciously for days on end, he was incapable even of opening a book. When he came in, Eloise was watching television, newspaper in hand in order not to miss one of those estimable programs, and she jumped up, all smiles, to give him a welcoming kiss: a welcome which he found exaggerated and absurd, very much "the little woman." He went over to the bar, or rather to the cart which served as a bar, and poured himself a whiskey that he didn't want. Then he sat down in a chair which was the twin of Eloise's, and stared at the little screen with an attentive air. Eloise tore her gaze away long enough to turn to him and ask:

"Had a good day?"

"Fine. And you?"

"Me too."

Seemingly relieved, she glued herself once more to the set. An unknown young couple were trying to make a word out of a jumble of wooden letters handed them by a sweetly smiling quizmistress. Gilles lit a cigarette and closed his eyes.

"I think it's 'pharmacy,' " said Eloise.

"What?"

"I think the word they're looking for is 'pharmacy.' "

"Very likely," he said.

He closed his eyes again. Then he tried a mouthful of his drink. It was already warm. He put it down again on the pile carpet.

"Nicholas called. He wanted to know if we'd like to meet

him at the Club tonight. What do you think?"

"Let's wait and see," he said, "I've only just come in."

"Otherwise, there's some cold veal in the fridge. And there's a serial on TV."

"Great," he thought. "A nice choice. Either I can have dinner with Nicholas who will tell me for the umpteenth time that his masterpiece would have been filmed ages ago if the film world wasn't so corrupt. Or I can sit in my armchair watching an asinine program and eating cold veal. What a ghastly prospect!" And yet in the old days he used to go out, see his friends, enjoy himself, meet new people: every night was a ball! Where were his friends now? He knew perfectly well where they were, and he had only to reach for the telephone. *They* had simply grown tired of telephoning him during the past three months. But try as he might, he could not think of a single name, a single face he wanted to see. Only that windbag Nicholas hung on, for the simple reason that he needed someone to pay for his drinks.

The telephone rang and he made no move. There had been a time when he would have leaped to answer it, confident that love or fortune or adventure awaited him. But now it was Eloise who answered it. She shouted from the bedroom:

"It's for you. It's Jean."

He hesitated for a moment. What was he to say to him?

Then it struck him that he had been very rude that morning and that it was stupid and shameful to be rude. After all, it was he who had burdened the poor chap with his troubles and then left him standing in the middle of the street. He picked up the receiver.

"Hello, Gilles. Are you all right?"

"Yes," he said.

Jean's voice was warm, anxious, the voice of a real friend. Gilles was touched.

"I'm terribly sorry about this morning," he began, "I . . ."

"We'll go into all that tomorrow," said Jean. "What are you doing tonight?"

"I think I'm . . . we're going to stay here," he said, "and eat some cold veal."

It was a barely disguised cry for help, and there was a momentary silence. Then Jean said gently:

"You ought to go out, you know. There's the first night at the Bobino, if you like. I've got some seats, I . . ."

"No, thanks," said Gilles. "I'm not very keen to go out. We'll make a real night of it tomorrow, if you like."

It was not what he meant, and Jean knew it. But Jean was late; he still had to change and go out again, and it suited him to take Gilles at his word. He acquiesced, said, "Good night, Gilles," in a voice that was more affectionate than usual, and hung up. Gilles felt more alone than ever. He went back to the living room and sat down again. Eloise was still riveted to the television. Suddenly it got on his nerves, and he blurted out:

"How can you watch that?"

Instead of showing surprise, she turned towards him with a gentle, forlorn, resigned expression.

"I thought it would give you an excuse not to talk to me."

For a moment he was so astonished that he made no reply. At the same time, the humility of her words filled him with a secret dread with which he was only too familiar—the dread of hurting people. And he felt he had been unmasked.

"Why do you say that?"

She shrugged.

"Because. I think . . . I have the feeling that you want to be left alone, that you don't want me to fuss over you. So I watch television."

She looked at him imploringly, longing for him to say, "But of course I want you to fuss over me, to talk to me." And for a moment he was tempted to do so, just to please her. But it would have been a lie, yet another lie, and he did not even have the right to ask her.

"I'm not very well at the moment," he said in a weak voice. "Don't be cross with me. I don't know what's the matter."

"I'm not cross with you," she said, "I know what it's like. I had the same thing when I was twenty-two. A depression. I used to cry all the time. My mother was at her wits' end."

Of course, the inevitable comparison! Eloise had always had everything.

"And how did it resolve itself?"

His voice was harsh, sarcastic. He really could not bring himself to compare "his" illness with Eloise's. He found it almost insulting.

"It went away suddenly, just like that. I took some little pills for a month—it's stupid, I can't remember what they were called. And one morning, I felt better."

She was being quite serious. He looked at her with a sort of hatred.

"It's a pity you've forgotten what they were called. Perhaps you could ring up your mother and ask her."

She got up, came over to him, and took his head in her hands. He gazed at the calm, beautiful face, the lips he had so often kissed, the blue eyes full of compassion.

"Gilles, Gilles, I know that I'm not very bright and that I'm not much use to you. But I love you, Gilles darling. . . ."

She was weeping now, clinging to his jacket, and he·was overcome with pity and at the same time an immense boredom.

"Don't cry," he said. "Don't cry, everything will be all right. I'm in a bad way; I'll go and see a doctor tomorrow."

And as her sobs gradually subsided, like those of a frightened child, he promised her he would see a doctor the next day, ate up his cold veal with a good grace, and tried to talk to her a little. Then he kissed her tenderly on the cheek and turned over on his side in the double bed, praying that the dawn would never come.

4

The doctor was intelligent, which did not help matters. On the contrary. He had examined Gilles with a stethoscope and asked a series of banal questions with the impatient air of a man who is under no illusions about the tricks of his trade. Now Gilles was sitting opposite him in a big Louis XIII armchair, gazing intently at him in the vague hope that his purposefulness and self-assurance did not conceal a total inability to cure him. "I suppose he affects a confident doctor's look, just as there are earnest lawyer's looks, just as even I must sometimes have a keen, intelligent journalist's look." But he could not suppress a glimmer of hope. Perhaps there existed a little pill somewhere which could cure life-sickness? Why not? Perhaps he only needed a little more calcium or iron or God-knows-what in order to be happy. These things existed, after all! We are always boasting about our brain power and our will power and our self-sufficiency and then we find ourselves paralyzed because we lack vitamin B. Yes, that was what one had to tell oneself; that was what one had to admit. A body is no more than a delicate piece of machinery and . . .

"So you're not feeling well," said the doctor. "I'm afraid I can't pretend that there's much I can do about it."

"What do you mean?"

Gilles felt angry and humiliated. For the past hour, he had virtually thrown himself on this man's mercy, had put his trust in him, and now the charlatan was calmly telling him that he was going to let him down. He was supposed to be a doctor, after all, it was his job. He "must" do something. Suppose garage mechanics no longer knew anything about cars; suppose . . .

"Physically, you're in good shape. At least, so it seems. I can do some tests, if you like. Or give you a prescription for a tonic. One capsule before every meal, which you'll take once every five . . ."

His tone was almost mocking, and Gilles hated him. He had been looking for a friendly father figure, and he'd found a blasé scientist.

"If you think it'll do me any good, I'm perfectly capable of taking some medicine twice a day," he said drily.

The doctor laughed.

"What medicine? You're suffering from the kind of generalized *atonia* which is called depression. It's mental, sexual, etc.; just as described to me. I can send you to a psychiatrist, if you like. Sometimes it works, sometimes not. There's a Doctor Giraut who is very good. . . ."

Gilles dismissed the idea with a wave of his hand.

"I could tell you to travel, or rest, or bury yourself in work. I'm not a good doctor when it comes to such things, I admit.

I can't tell you what I don't know. I can only advise you to be patient."

With that, he called in a secretary and dictated a prescription at once innocuous and complicated, as though he were offering Gilles a present. On second thought, he had a good face, intelligent and world-weary. He signed the slip and handed it to Gilles.

"You can always try this. At any rate, it'll reassure your wife, if you have one."

Gilles stood up, and hesitated. He wanted to say, "But what am I supposed to do?" He so seldom saw a doctor that this man's casualness amazed him.

"Thank you," he said. "I know you're very busy and that it was Jean who . . ."

"Jean is one of my best friends," the doctor said. "Anyway, my dear fellow, I see a dozen men like you every week. They usually get over it. It's the times we live in, as they say."

He patted Gilles on the back and steered him out of the door. It was five o'clock in the afternoon, and he found himself standing on the pavement, as dazed as a man who has just been told he hasn't long to live, but also furious. It was true that Jean had said to him, "Go and see this doctor, at least he won't tell you a pack of lies." But did a man in his profession have the right to tell one the unvarnished truth? He realized that he would have preferred some lying soothsayer or pill pusher. He had sunk so low that he would have preferred being cheated, lied to, anything, so long as it was comforting. That was what he had come to, and his self-disgust redoubled at the thought.

What was he to do now? He could always look in at the paper, although for once he had a good excuse for being absent. "Please, sir, I've been to the doctor." This childishness, this habit of making excuses and telling lies, of treating other adults as schoolmasters easily gulled, this whole attitude of his depressed him more and more. And as for his work, which he used to care about so passionately that he literally felt incapable of doing it badly, Jean was doing everything for him at the moment, and sooner or later it would be noticed. He would be thrown out, fired from the newspaper he loved, the newspaper he had fought so hard to get on; he would have to go back to being a hack on some scandal sheet or other, and he would have only himself to blame. It was inescapable. He would end up with the squalid bums certain newspapers are full of, would drink himself silly, and would spend his evenings weeping with self-pity in night clubs.

Well, if he was going to go to the dogs he might as well begin at once. Gilda should be at home, Gilda would think of something. Gilda was always there, ready to cater to the pleasure of others, or her own, or both at once. For years she had been kept by an amiable Brazilian who was fascinated by her cynicism, and she seldom if ever left her ground-floor flat in Passy, immured in pleasure as others are in opium. At forty-eight she was still physically superb, with a leonine head, a face with scarcely a wrinkle, and an appalling temper. Jean used to say of her that she was one of the last remaining Barbey d'Aurevilly characters and Gilles might well have agreed had he not, being a better judge of women, discerned at times behind that triumphant mask a suggestion of playacting, rather facile and bookish. However that might be, Gilda was a good sort and she was fond of him. He hailed a taxi—for the past two months, the idea of driving his Simca around Paris had seemed an unimaginable ordeal—and gave Gilda's address.

She was alone for once, dressed in one of the elaborately

embroidered dressing gowns which were her specialty, and she welcomed Gilles with a flood of endearments and reproaches. He sat on the edge of the bed and listened to her. She had missed him. She was just back from the Bahamas. She hated the tropics almost as much as she hated the snow. She had a new lover of nineteen with whom she was playing at "Cheri." But his sister attracted her too. Would he have a whiskey or a martini? He had always drunk martinis during their time together. How many days had it lasted, by the way? She had almost fallen in love with him. For good. At the end of ten minutes she drew breath and gave him a searching look.

"*I* think *you're* sickening for something."

They burst out laughing. It had always been a pet expression of theirs: *I* think *you're* getting the flu. On edge at first, Gilles relaxed now, stretching out his legs and taking in the baroque contents of the room with the casual and affectionate eye of an ex-tenant.

"I've just seen a doctor," he said.

"You? What's wrong with you? It's true you've lost weight. You haven't got? . . ."

The word was left in midair, and Gilles thought ironically that it was probably the only word which could still shock Gilda.

"No, I haven't got cancer. There's nothing wrong with me. I'm just feeling low."

"Oh, that," she said. "You frightened me at first. How long has it been going on?"

"Er . . . about three months. I don't really know."

"That," she said sagely, "isn't just feeling low. That's acute depression. Remember the state I was in in '62?"

The tiresome thing about this malady, he was beginning

to realize, was that, first of all, everyone had had it, and secondly, everyone found it passionately interesting to talk about. So Gilles listened to the story of Gilda's depression—which, it seemed, had miraculously come to an end one fine morning in Capri—vaguely trying to find some point of similarity with what he himself felt, and failing utterly.

"I know what you're thinking," Gilda said suddenly. "You're thinking that in your case it's different. But you're wrong. It's just the same. One of these days you'll either wake up feeling as gay as a lark, the way you used to, or you'll put a bullet through your head. You're more intelligent than I am, agreed, but what good is that to you at the moment, I'd like to know?"

She spoke tenderly, her hand on his knee, her splendid body leaning towards him, and he was amazed that he did not desire her. He had always wanted her every time he saw her. He reached out toward her breasts, but she stopped his hand midway.

"No," she said, "I can see you don't want to."

Instead, he stretched out alongside her, fully dressed, and she drew his head onto her shoulder. He lay there motionless, and she stroked his hair in silence. With his face buried in the silk of her negligee, he felt uncomfortable, found it difficult to breathe, but was incapable of moving. Eventually, she shook him and he uttered a low groan.

"Listen, Gilles, Arnaut will be here soon. I have to get dressed, he wants to take me to some frightful night club or other. But stay and make yourself at home. And if you like, I'll send Véronique round to you. She's Indian, superb looking, and one of the most versatile women I know. It'll take your mind off things. Are you still with your Eloise?"

Her voice had at once taken on that disdainful tone of

women who disapprove of protracted relationships for their ex-lovers. He nodded.

"Well, is it yes or no?"

His only desire was to stay where he was. Not to have to plunge back into the maelstrom of Paris at seven o'clock in the evening and look for a taxi.

"Yes," he said.

He watched her with real pleasure as she changed, put the finishing touches to her make-up, made a telephone call. He even gave young Arnaut, who was the perfect little gigolo, an affectionate handshake—though not without a certain condescension.

Waiting for an unknown woman in this barely remembered flat, he felt rather like the hero of a detective story, and the idea amused him. Once they had left, he stretched out on the drawing-room sofa in a man's dressing gown, which someone had miraculously left behind, lit a cigarette, picked up a magazine, placed a drink beside him on the floor, had to get up to fetch an ashtray, had to get up again to open the window because he was suffocating, had to get up to close it again because he felt cold, had to get up to turn down the soft music which Gilda had left playing not softly enough, had to get up to look for his cigarettes which he had left in Gilda's bedroom, had to get up to put an ice cube in his lukewarm whiskey, had to get up again to change the record after it had played for the third consecutive time, had to get up to answer the telephone, once only, had to get up to change magazines. By the time the doorbell rang at the end of an hour, he was in a state of such total exasperation with himself that he did not get up to answer it.

5

He was walking through the streets now, heading vaguely toward his flat but making enormous detours, incapable of stopping, incapable of going home. There was a great buzzing emptiness in his head, and it seemed to him that everyone was staring at him, that everyone found him as ugly and shabby as he felt. One minute he seemed to be making no progress, the next he had crossed an entire square without even noticing. Finding himself in the Tuileries, he remembered Drieu La Rochelle and his so-called last walk there: he himself, he thought bitterly, would never have the courage nor the desire to commit suicide. Not even that. His was a despair that could stand any epithet except courageous or romantic. He would almost have preferred to want to kill himself. He would have preferred anything as long as it was drastic enough.

"But perhaps that's how I'll end up after all," he told himself as though by way of consolation. "Surely if this goes on I won't be able to stand it much longer. . . . I shall have to do something about it." And he thought of this "I" with a mixture of hope and fear as of some stranger endowed with the possibility of acting in his stead. But it would have to wait; for at this moment there was nothing, no one, inside him capable of seizing a gun and firing it into his mouth or of throwing his body into the dark-green Seine below. He could no more imagine his death than his life, and this simply left him where he was, breathing, existing, suffering.

He shivered and decided to go get drunk at the Club. It wasn't much of a solution, but he could not go on tramping the streets like this, his icy hands jammed in the pockets of his raincoat, his body, his shoulders, his heart, his lungs strung together on taut, twitching wires. He would get dead drunk and someone would take him home. At least he would sleep, and Eloise would look after him.

At the Club, he greeted the barman, slapped Joel on the back, exchanged a quick joke with Pierre, waved to André, Bill, Zoé—in short, did everything that was expected of him and, ignoring various invitations, sat down alone at the bar. He drank one Scotch, then another, with the feeling that he might just as well have been drinking water. At that moment Thomas arrived, visibly drunk, lucky man, and sat down beside him. They had been intimate enemies on the paper for the past four years as a result of some dreary quarrel involving a girl and a story the details of which Gilles had forgotten. Thomas was short, thin, and sharp-featured, with a high-pitched voice that got on Gilles's nerves.

"Well, well, here's our pretty boy!" he exclaimed, breathing whiskey fumes into Gilles's face so that he retreated involuntarily. No question about it, this was all he needed to round off the evening.

"What are you moving away for? Don't you like me? Go on, say so, if you don't like me. . . ."

Pierre was signaling from the other end of the room. He was in charge of the Club at night, and he was making signs to Gilles that the other was drunk, a fact which was only too obvious. Thomas went on insistently:

"Well, pretty boy? Aren't you going to answer?"

Suddenly, with a movement which might or might not have been deliberate, he upset his drink down Gilles's shirt front. The glass crashed to the floor and everyone stopped talking.

At the same moment, something snapped inside Gilles. It was as though, at long last, his will to happiness, his respect for other people, his self-control, everything seemed to be crumbling, disappearing beneath the upsurge of his rage, and he found himself hitting Thomas—who, poor fellow, had been floored by the first blow. He found himself on his knees, punching the sharp-featured face, punching life, punching his disappointment with life, punching himself, while violent hands grasped him by the shoulders and pulled him backward and he still flailed away, almost sobbing, until a hard blow landed on his mouth just as the words "mad dog" reached his ears. After he had stopped struggling, there was a silence, and he saw a circle of horrified, uncomprehending faces around him, saw little Thomas on the floor getting up on his hands and knees, and tasted the salt mixture of blood and tears on his lip. He backed out slowly, and no one said a word to him. Not even Pierre, with whom he'd gotten drunk all during his youth. In fact, he realized, it was Pierre who had hit him, and he had been right to do it. It was his job, after all. We all have to earn a living.

When he got home he could hear voices in the flat, and

he paused in surprise on the threshold. It was almost mid-night. He took out his handkerchief and wiped the dried blood from his mouth: he did not want to make an entrance like something out of *Frankenstein*. In the old days he would have been unable to resist it, but he had lost his appetite for such pranks. Jean was in the sitting room with his girl-friend Marthe, a plump, stupid, tender-hearted brunette, and Eloise was looking out of the window. She gave a start as he entered, and Jean turned towards him with an expression of deliberate composure, while Marthe screamed:

"Good God, Gilles! What have you done to yourself?"

"It's a real family council," he thought. "Tried and true friends worriedly waiting with the faithful companion . . . and then, as a crowning stroke of luck, the hero returns wounded." Eloise was already flying to the bathroom in search of cotton.

He flopped into a chair and grinned.

"I had a fight," he said, "a stupid fight . . . like all fights. Guess who with, Jean? With Thomas!"

"Thomas? Don't tell me Thomas did that!"

Jean gave the incredulous chuckle of a keen boxing fan.

"No," said Gilles. "It was Pierre, while he was separating us."

He was suddenly appalled by that stupid quarrel, by the ferocity and viciousness that had taken possession of him. It was bad enough hating himself, but if he became hateful to others . . . He raised his hand.

"Let's not talk about it any more. Tomorrow they'll give me a bad time at the paper and by the next day they'll have forgotten all about it. To what do I owe the pleasure of see-ing you?"

He directed the question at Marthe, who smiled back

amiably without replying. Jean must have said to her, "Gilles is in a bad way," and she gazed at him with the interested look of someone for whom such a condition was plainly inconceivable. Eloise had now returned, and with the grim, purposeful air women assume in the role of nurse, she tilted his head back.

"Keep still. This will sting a bit, but only for a moment."

"Now she's Mother," he thought. "My little boy has been up to mischief." What do they all think they're doing with their clumsy routines? Back there, it had been a charade about masculine chivalry: you don't go around beating up midgets! Now I arrive home in the middle of a conference about my welfare. Jean's playing the tough guy whose pal has been in a fight, Eloise the domesticated little woman, and Marthe—Marthe's doing nothing because she's incapable of doing anything. Otherwise she'd be warming the alcohol and holding it for Eloise. . . ."

As a matter of fact, it stung badly. He grunted.

"Well," said Jean, "what did Daniel have to say?"

"Daniel?"

"The doctor."

"Didn't you call him?"

He had said this casually, as a sarcastic dig at Jean's behavior towards him over the years—paternal, patronizing, and slightly meddlesome—and he realized, seeing Jean blush, that he had scored a bull's-eye. So Jean really was worried. He was suddenly afraid, with a hideous, animal fear: what if he were to end up in an asylum?

"Yes," Jean said, with the pious air of a man who won't tell a lie—because he knows it is too late—"yes, I rang him up."

"Were you worried?"

"A little. Anyway, he reassured me."

"So much so that you're here at midnight?"

Jean suddenly lost his temper.

"The reason I'm here is because Eloise was out of her mind with worry; she knew you were seeing the doctor at four o'clock, and she'd had no news since. I came to keep her company and reassure her. I talked to Daniel: you're overwrought, overtired, and depressed like nine-tenths of the population of Paris. But that's no reason to leave people worrying about you or to get into fights in bars with Thomas or anyone else."

There was a silence. Gilles smiled.

"Yes, papa. What else did your doctor friend have to say?"

"That you needed a change of air."

"Ah! I suppose the paper will offer me a cruise to the Bahamas. Will you talk to the boss for me?"

He knew he was being stupid and unpleasant and not even funny, but he could not help himself.

"I'm told it's lovely in the Bahamas," Marthe, innocent as ever, observed with a worldly air, and Jean gave her such a furious look that Gilles had an uncontrollable urge to laugh. He bit his lip until it hurt, but he felt the laughter welling up inside him, inexorably, like his recent outburst of violence. He made a desperate effort, taking deep breaths, but Marthe's remark went round and round in his head, irresistibly comic. He spluttered, closed his eyes, and suddenly erupted in a gale of laughter.

He laughed and laughed until he nearly choked. "The Bahamas, the Bahamas," he kept murmuring between bouts, as though to excuse himself. And as soon as he opened his eyes, the three dismayed faces confronting him made him laugh even more. The cut on his lip had reopened, he could feel a trickle of blood on his chin, and he thought wildly that he must look like a madman, bleeding and sobbing with laughter in the middle of the night in a ribbed velvet armchair. Everything had become miraculously absurd, side-splittingly funny. My God, what a day! And the afternoon! Sitting like a pasha in a borrowed dressing gown, waiting for a woman he hadn't even opened the door to! . . . If he could only tell Jean that one. But he was laughing too much, he couldn't get a word out. He was howling with laughter. Screwy, that's what life was, screwy. Why couldn't the others over there see the joke?

"Stop it," said Jean, "stop it."

"He's going to slap my face, I know it," Gilles thought. "He thinks that's the thing to do on these occasions. Every-one thinks there's a right thing to do in every situation in life. If you laugh too much you get slapped in the face, if you cry too much you're put to sleep, or else you get sent to the Bahamas."

But Jean did not slap his face. He had opened the window, the women had taken refuge in the bedroom, and now his laughter was subsiding. He no longer knew why he had been laughing. Any more than he knew why warm tears were now pouring down his face in an unceasing, silent stream, or why Jean's hand was trembling as he handed him a red-and-blue-checked handkerchief.

33

PART TWO

Limoges

6

He was lying in the grass on his stomach, watching the sun rise over the hill beyond. Ever since he had come down here he had been sleeping badly and waking up too early, as worn out by the quiet of the countryside as he had been by the frenzy of Paris. His sister, with whom he was staying, knew it and was obscurely annoyed by it. She was childless and Gilles had always been like a son to her. Not having been able to "get him back on his feet," as she put it, within a fortnight was, in her view, a direct insult to the Limousin, the fresh air, and the family in general. Of course she had read about these "nervous depressions" in the newspapers, but she put them down to moodiness rather than illness. As full of goodness as she was devoid of imagination, for forty years Odile had divided her life equally between her parents and then her husband and her household chores, and she found it impossible to believe that there was anything that could not be cured by rest, thick steaks, and country walks. Meanwhile Gilles continued to get thinner and more taciturn; occasionally he vanished from the room when, for instance, she was discussing the latest news with her husband, Florent. And if she happened to turn on the television—a marvelous set with two channels, which they had just bought—he shut himself up in his room and did not reappear until the following day. He had always been baffling, but this time, Paris had sent him completely off the rails. Poor Gilles . . . Sometimes she would run her fingers through his hair; surprisingly he would let her do so, even sitting at her feet while she did her knitting, often without saying a word, as though he found a momentary comfort in her presence. She would chat to him about things which, she vaguely sensed, did not interest him but nevertheless calmed him by their very ordinariness: the seasons, the crops, the neighbors.

He had decided to go away on the morning after that dreadful day in Paris, and since he was up to his ears in debt and, moreover, terrified of facing strangers, he had taken refuge with Odile in the rather tumble-down house which had been left to them by their parents and in which she had lived ever since with the gentle Florent, a lawyer but a man presumably as incapable of fighting a lawsuit as of fathering a child, leading a life as remote from actuality as it was possible to imagine, thanks to a few farm rents and dividends. Of course he knew he would be bored to death, but at least he would be protected against himself and those ridiculous outbursts which, he felt instinctively, would become more and more frequent if he remained in Paris; and at least, if he rolled about on the ground, it would be in front of only the local sheep, who would be less embarrassed than his friends or his mistress. Moreover, relations with his sister, his own flesh and blood, were easy, and this seemed to him a blessing in itself; he had a horror of any sort of emotionalism or demonstrativeness. Nor need he feel any guilt about anyone. He had left Eloise in the flat, Jean at the paper, with a firm promise to return cured within a month. A fortnight had already gone by, and he was in utter despair. The country-side was beautiful but he knew it without feeling it; the house was familiar but he was at home in it without being attuned to it; and each tree, each wall, each passage seemed to be saying to him, "You were happy here once, life was good," as he slunk along the pathways or the corridors like a thief—a thief who had, himself, been robbed of every-thing, even his childhood.

The sun had now risen and was beginning to bathe the meadow in its warmth. He buried his face in the wet grass, turning his head from side to side, slowly, sniffing the earth, deliberately trying to recapture the delicious sensation of well-being it had once given him. But even such simple pleasures could not be summoned on command, and he re-coiled with self-disgust from the histrionic gestures of a bogus nature lover, like a man in bed with a woman he no longer loves, using the same words and gestures that be-longed to their former passion, but without feeling, and sud-denly aghast. He got up, noticing with mild irritation that his sweater was soaking wet, and made his way back to the house.

It was an old gray house with a blue tiled roof and two comic little gables, a typical Limousin house with a terrace in front and a hill behind, the sort of house which smelled of lime trees and summer and dusk no matter what the season or the time of day. At least, so it had always seemed to him, even now in the early morning light as, shivering slightly, he entered the kitchen. Odile was already up, in her dressing gown, making the coffee. He kissed her, and she muttered something about people getting pneumonia from rolling about in the morning dew. Nevertheless, he felt better for being near her, sniffing the fragrance of coffee, of her eau de Cologne, and of wood smoke from the big fireplace, thinking how he would like to be the big marmalade cat who was stretching himself on the dresser, having just decided to wake up. The simple, homely pleasures of country life! What a pity such clichés could only sustain him for a few minutes at a time before life and his obsession caught up with him again like a pack of hounds in full cry which has given the stag a few minutes' breathing space only in order to prolong the hunt.

At this point Florent appeared, also in his dressing gown. He was short and fat like his wife, but with enormous blue eyes like pools of water oddly out of place in his baby face. He also had a curious habit of miming everything that was said: he would shield his face with his arm if there was talk of war, put a finger to his lips if there was talk of love, and so on. Now, on seeing Gilles, he raised his arm high in salute and greeted him as though they were a hundred yards apart.

"Slept well, my dear fellow? Pleasant dreams?"

This was followed by a conspiratorial wink. He obstinately refused to attribute Gilles's present state to anything more complicated than an unhappy love affair, and none of Gilles's denials had made the slightest difference. In his eyes, Gilles was a seducer who for once had allowed some slut to get the better of him. So that if, for example, he found Gilles slumped in an armchair, he would let fall some clever phrase like: "There are lots more fish in the ocean," frenziedly waving all ten fingers in the air as he did so. On these occasions, Gilles, torn between rage and hilarity, made no reply. But when he thought about it, he experienced a sort of pleasure at being thus misunderstood, a sort of comfort. After all, it might have been true. By confusing things, it somehow minimized them. Like a man stricken with jaundice and lying in bed with a face the color of a lemon while one of his friends sympathizes with him about signs of incipient baldness.

"What time is it?" asked Florent cheerfully. "Eight o'clock? What a lovely day!"

Gilles looked out of the window with a shudder. What a lovely day was in store for him, indeed! He would shortly drive his sister to the village to do the shopping; he would buy cigarettes and the newspapers, come back and read on the terrace before lunch, and try without success to have a siesta after it. Then, without wanting to in the least, he would go for a stroll in the wood, have a whiskey with Florent before dinner when he got back, and then retire to bed early, too early, so that his sister, who had been champing at the bit since eight o'clock, could switch on the television at long last. It struck him that there might be a touch of affectation in his abhorrence of the box, he couldn't think why. He felt a twinge of remorse: what right had he to deprive his sister of this pleasure, however deadly it might seem to him. Her life wasn't as gay as all that. He leaned toward her:

"I'll stay and watch television with you tonight."

"Oh, no," she said, "not tonight. We're going to the Rouargues'! I told you the other day."

"In that case," he said jokingly, "I'll stay and watch it by myself."

Odile jumped. "Are you crazy? You're coming! Madame

Rouargue made a special point of it. She's known you since you were five."

"I didn't come here to go to parties," complained Gilles, horrified, "I came here for a rest. I won't go!"

"Yes you will . . . rude . . . heartless . . . little wretch. . . ."

They were yelling at each other, suddenly recapturing the tone of their childhood quarrels, while Florent, appalled, produced a variety of appeasing gestures, now imitating with both arms a conductor desperately trying to keep up with his orchestra, now wagging one finger like an earnest preacher. All to no avail for a good five minutes, during which Gilles's mother, his dissolute life, respect for the proprieties, and Odile's innate stupidity were variously invoked. At this final shaft from Gilles his sister burst into tears; whereupon Florent took her in his arms, after a comical show of shadow-boxing in Gilles's direction, and Gilles, shattered, conscience-stricken, put his arms around her in his turn and promised to go wherever she wished. He was acknowledged, by way of reward, to be a good boy at heart. And so, at eight o'clock that evening, they climbed into Florent's ancient Citroën, which he drove in so bizarre a fashion that for the twenty-mile journey into Limoges Gilles had no time to worry about anything except his life.

7

There were still some blue drawing rooms in Limoges, although they had become increasingly rare. Many years before, a general craze for blue velvet upholstery had seized the town and certain families, either from financial necessity or fidelity to tradition, had kept them. The Rouargues were one of these, and as he entered their drawing room Gilles had the impression of walking back into his childhood; an endless sequence of tea parties rose before his eyes, hours of boredom spent sitting on a pouf waiting for his parents, hours of daydreaming against a background of faded blue. But already his hostess, all pink and white, was pressing him to her bosom.

"Gilles, my little Gilles. I haven't seen you for twenty years. But we always read your articles, you know, my husband and I, we haven't quite lost touch with you. Of course, we don't necessarily agree with what you write, because we've always been a bit reactionary" (she added this as though to indicate a minor quirk) "but we follow you. Will you be with us long? A touch of anemia, Odile tells me. Such a pleasure to have you! Come and let me introduce you to everybody."

Dazed and jostled, Gilles allowed himself to be kissed, fondled, and made much of by the old lady. The room was full of people, all of them standing except for three old gentlemen perched on chairs, and Gilles began to feel the onset of panic. He glanced angrily in his sister's direction, but she was in her element, scudding through the room in full sail and flinging her arms around total strangers. "How long is it since my father died, fifteen years ago? What on earth am I doing here?" He followed the old lady, bending over a dozen hands, shaking a dozen more, trying to smile each time, but barely glancing at these unfamiliar faces, even though some of the women were attractive and well-dressed. Finally he sat down, taking refuge beside one of the old gentlemen, who told him he had been one of his father's oldest friends and asked him what he thought of the political situation before proceeding to explain it to him. Gilles was leaning over him slightly, pretending to listen, when Madame Rouargue took him by the sleeve.

"Edmond," she ordered, "stop monopolizing our young friend. Gilles, I want you to meet Madame Silvener. Nathalie, this is Gilles Lantier."

Gilles turned and found himself face to face with a tall, handsome, smiling woman. She had bold green eyes and red hair, and there was something at once arrogant and open-hearted in her expression. She smiled at him, said "Good evening" in a low voice, and moved away immediately. He looked after her, intrigued. In this little blue drawing room, faded and antiquated, her flamelike presence seemed oddly out of place.

"It's a question of prestige," the garrulous Edmond went on. . . . "Ah, you're looking at the beautiful Madame Silvener? She's the queen of our little circle. If only I were your age! But as I was saying, the foreign policy of a country such as ours . . ."

Dinner was interminable. From time to time Gilles noticed the beautiful Madame Silvener looking toward him from the other end of the table with a calm, thoughtful expression that contrasted with her general behavior. She talked a good deal, there was a good deal of laughter all round her, and Gilles watched her with a tinge of irony. She evidently did see herself as the queen of Limoges society and wanted to make an impression on this unknown Parisian, a journalist to boot. There was a time when he would have been slightly diverted by a fortnight's affair with the wife of a provincial bigwig, and would have given a splendid Balzacian account of it to his friends when he got back. But now he did not feel the slightest inclination. He looked down at his hands, lying thin and useless on the tablecloth, and wanted only to get up and leave.

After dinner, he clung to Odile's side like a child, and she, seeing his drawn features, his trembling hands, and the almost imploring expression in his eyes, for the first time felt really afraid for him. She made her excuses to Madame Rouargue and, towing the slightly tipsy Florent behind them, they slipped away without further ceremony, or as little as is possible on a social occasion in the provinces. Gilles sat hunched in the back of the car, shivering and biting his nails. Never again, he swore to himself, would he undertake another such expedition.

As for Nathalie Silvener, she had fallen in love with him at first sight.

8

Gilles was fishing. Or, to be more exact, he was lazily watching as Florent, with all the guile he could muster, offered some revolting maggots to fish that were far more cunning than himself. It was nearly noon, the weather was hot and they were both in shirt sleeves; for the first time since he could remember, Gilles felt a sort of well-being. The water was astonishingly clear and, lying face downward, he could see the round stones on the river bed and the merry dance of the fish as they darted toward his brother-in-law's hook, delicately nibbled off the bait, and glided smugly away, while Florent snapped his rod in the empty air with a violent oath.

"Your hooks are too big," said Gilles.

"They're made especially for gudgeon," said Florent crossly. "Why don't you have a try, instead of sneering?"

47

"No thanks," said Gilles, "I'm very comfortable as I am. Look, who's this?"

He started up in alarm: a woman was coming down the path to the river and making straight for them. He looked around for somewhere to hide, but the grassy banks were smooth and bare. The sun glinted on the woman's hair, and he recognized her at once.

"It's Nathalie Silvener!" Florent exclaimed, blushing violently.

"Are you in love with her?" teased Gilles, receiving in reply a look of such fury he said no more. She had drawn closer to them now, making a charming picture in the sunlight, erect and smiling, her eyes greener than the other evening.

"Odile sent me. I promised the other day I would stop by, and I kept my word. How's the fishing going?"

Both men had risen to their feet and Florent gestured ruefully towards his pail, in which there lay a solitary suicide. She burst out laughing and turned to Gilles.

"What about you? Or are you just an observer?"

He laughed without replying. She sat down on the ground beside them. In her brown leather skirt, brown pullover, and low-heeled shoes, she looked much younger than before. Not so much the *femme fatale*. She must be about thirty-five, Gilles guessed. He found her less forbidding or, more precisely, she seemed no longer a stranger.

"Come on, show me what you can do," she commanded Florent, who went through the same motions as before. They watched in awed silence as the float bobbed beneath the surface, Florent jerked up his rod, and the hook dangled empty at the end of his line. Gilles roared with laughter as Florent threw his rod to the ground and pretended to jump on it.

"I've had enough, I'm going back," he said. "I'll make you an eggnog, if you like."

"An eggnog?" asked Gilles. "Do they still exist?"

They laughed again as they watched Florent clamber up the path laden with his two rods, his folding stool, and his rucksack; then he disappeared and they were left alone, suddenly at a loss. Gilles snatched a blade of grass and put it between his teeth. He could feel this woman's eyes upon him, and thought vaguely that perhaps all he had to do was to reach out and take her. She would either slap his face or kiss him, he didn't know which. But something would happen, he was sure of that. The trouble was that he had lost the knack of dealing with equivocal situations; in Paris, everything was only too open, obvious, clear-cut. He cleared his throat and looked up. She was looking at him pensively, as she had during that disastrous dinner party the night before last.

"Are you a good friend of my sister's?"

"No. To tell you the truth, she was amazed to see me." She stopped. "Good," thought Gilles, "now she'll kiss me. Apparently they don't waste time in the provinces either." But there was something about this woman that inhibited his cynicism.

"Why did you come, then?"

"To see you," she replied, calmly. "I was attracted to you instantly the other night. I wanted to see you again."

"That's nice of you."

What Gilles found disconcerting was the gaiety, the calm in her voice. He was taken aback.

"When you left that party so suddenly the other night, everyone started gossiping—about you, your life, your depression. They were fascinated. Freud is always fascinating, especially in the provinces."

"So you came to see the symptoms firsthand?"

He was furious now—both at being talked about as though he were an invalid and at her telling him about it so breezily.

"I told you I came to see *you*. I couldn't care less about your illness. Let's go and have that eggnog."

She jumped to her feet while he remained lying where he was, suddenly annoyed at the interruption. He looked at her from beneath his eyelashes with a sulky expression which he knew rather suited him, and suddenly, with the same abrupt quickness, she knelt beside him, taking his head between her hands and smiling mysteriously into his face.

"You're too thin," she said.

They gazed into each other's eyes. "If she kisses me, that's that," Gilles thought. "I won't be able to see her again. But it would be a pity." All these stupid ideas were mixed up in his mind, and his heart was suddenly beating faster. But she was already on her feet again, brushing herself off without looking at him. He got up and followed her. He stopped for a moment on the path, and she turned around.

"Are you sure you're not a bit mad," he said.

All at once her face assumed a serious expression aging her ten years, and she shook her head.

"No, not at all."

They did not speak again until they reached the house. The eggnogs were cool, Odile was pink with excitement—for Nathalie was a celebrity—and Florent had put on a clean jacket. She stayed for half an hour, and was charming and talkative. It was Gilles who escorted her to her car. She would pick him up the following afternoon, because he was so anxious to see the Matisse exhibition at the municipal gallery. Gilles spent the rest of the day with a somber, furious face and went to bed even earlier than usual. "What's come over me? Why have I got myself involved with this woman? We'll end up in some country brothel near Limoges and I'm sure to be impotent. And I've committed myself to two hours of boredom in some museum tomorrow. I must be out of my mind." He woke up very early, his heart pounding with terror at the prospect, bitterly regretting the comfortable boredom which had been the pattern of his days. But they had no telephone and there was no way of putting Nathalie off.

9

"There," he said, "I hope you're pleased."

He had turned over on his back and was lying there
sweating, humiliated, out of breath; all the more humiliated
because he was being unfair and it was he who had practically dragged her into bed. They had had tea in an inn and
it was he who had bribed the manager into letting them
have this scruffy little room. She had not turned a hair when
he told her what he had done, she had not protested; nor
had she done anything to help him while he was vainly
exerting himself on top of her. She lay beside him now,
naked, calm, seemingly indifferent.

"Why should I be pleased? You seem so angry," she said
with a smile.

He bridled.

"It's never very pleasant for a man."

"Nor for a woman," she said quietly. "But you knew beforehand that it would be like that, and so, for that matter, did I. You took this room deliberately. You wanted to fail. Isn't that true?"

It was true enough. He laid his head on the bare shoulder beside him and closed his eyes. He felt exhausted, suddenly, and relaxed, as though he had really made love. How preposterous this room was, with its flowered curtains and that dreadful wardrobe. It was outside time, outside all reality. Like himself. Like the situation.

"Why did you accept?" he said meditatively, "if you knew . . ."

"I think I'm going to accept a lot of things from you," she answered.

There was a silence, then she murmured, "tell," and he began to tell her everything—Paris, Eloise, his friends, his job, the past months. It seemed to him that it would take years to tell it all. To define this "nothing." She listened to him without a word, simply lighting two cigarettes from time to time and passing him one. It must have been six or seven in the evening, but she did not seem to care. She did not touch him, did not stroke his hair, but lay motionless against him, her shoulder long since numb.

At last he fell silent and, vaguely ashamed, raised himself on one elbow to look at her. She gazed back at him without moving, her expression serious and thoughtful, and suddenly she smiled. "She's good, this woman," thought Gilles, "she's unbelievably good." And the idea of this perfect goodness available to him, the idea that someone should care about him so unreservedly, brought tears to his eyes. He bent over her in order to hide them, and gently kissed her smiling lips, her cheeks, her closed eyes. In the end he was not so impotent as all that. Nathalie's two hands clung to his shoulders.

Much later, he was to remember that it was the idea of her goodness which had allowed him to make love to her the first time. And he, who had never glimpsed anything remotely erotic in the finer feelings, for whom the phrase "she's a slut" would, if anything, have been vaguely exciting, would later, much later, too late in fact, prick up his ears when he overheard someone casually described as "a good woman." But now he looked at her and smiled, and apologized, not without a hint of self-satisfaction, for having been brutal. She was at the foot of the bed, dressing, and quickly turning her head toward him, interrupted.

"I can't pretend it was exactly enjoyable, but you feel better, don't you? Exorcized?"

He started, quick to anger.

"Are you always so honest?"

"No," she said, "it's the first time."

He began to laugh and got up in his turn. It was half past seven, and she must be late.

"Have you a dinner party tonight?"

"No, I'm dining at home. François will be getting worried."

"Who's François?"

"My husband."

He realized with amazement that he had never thought of her as married, that he knew nothing of her life, either past or present. Odile had embarked on a gossipy biography the other day, but he had not listened. He felt vaguely ashamed.

"I know nothing about you," he murmured.

"And I knew nothing about you an hour ago. I still don't know very much."

She smiled at him, and he stood for a moment transfixed by that smile. Now, right this very instant, was the time for him to finish the thing, if it had to be finished. And it had to be: he was incapable of loving anyone simply because he was incapable of loving himself. He was bound to make her suffer. No doubt he had only to make some slightly crude joke, something that would cause her to despise him. But he already shrank from doing so, and that smile of hers, steady, sincere, and full of promise, filled him with dread. He stammered:

"You know . . . I . . ."

"I know," she said calmly, "but I'm in love with you already."

He felt a flash of rebellion, of indignation even. This isn't the way the game is played: one simply didn't deliver oneself lock, stock, and barrel into the hands of a stranger! She was crazy. And how was he to get any pleasure from seducing her if she declared herself already seduced? How could he hope to love her if he had no doubts about her from the start? She spoiled everything! It was against all the rules. At the same time, he was fascinated by such prodigality, such lack of caution.

"How can you be sure?" he asked in the same light, careless tone of voice, and as he looked at her he suddenly thought how very beautiful she was, how made for love, and wondered whether she might not be teasing him. She looked him straight in the face and began to laugh.

"You're just as afraid it might be true as not, aren't you?" He nodded, secretly delighted at her having seen through him. "Well, it's true. Haven't you ever read any Russian novels? Where after two meetings one person suddenly says to the other, 'I love you'? And it's true; it takes the story straight to the final catastrophe."

"And what catastrophe do you predict for us, here in Limoges?"

"I don't know. But like the heroes of Russian novels, I don't care. Hurry up."

As they left together, he felt slightly reassured. A well-read woman is less of a nuisance, she knows more or less what to expect. The sun cast long, slanting shadows, bathing the new-mown hay in a glow of pink and gold, and he gazed at the profile of his new mistress with a certain satisfaction. After all, she was beautiful, the countryside too; he had proved himself a virile, if not an inspired, lover; and she said she loved him. Not bad for a neurotic. He began to laugh, and she turned her head toward him.

"Why are you laughing?"

"No reason. I'm happy."

She stopped the car, grasped him by the lapels, and shook him—all so quickly that he was completely taken aback.

"Say it again. Say it again. Say that you're happy."

Her voice had taken on a new tone—demanding, authoritative, sensual—and he felt a surge of desire for her. He took her by the wrists and kissed her hands, repeating, "I'm happy, I'm happy," with a new intensity, and she released him and drove on again in silence. They exchanged hardly another word on the drive home and she dropped him at the gate without their having made any plan to meet again. But that evening, lying in his bedroom, Gilles recalled that strange moment by the side of the road and thought, smiling to himself, it had seemed very much like real passion.

10

He had no news of her for several days, and was not surprised. He had been a casual adventure for her, an unsatisfactory one to boot, and she had spoken of love either out of convention—those bizarre bourgeois conventions—or out of whimsicality. Nevertheless, he was a little disappointed, and this accentuated his natural melancholy. He spoke little, shaved every other day, and tried to read a few books, preferably not Russian.

On the fifth day it was pouring rain in the afternoon and he was curled up, still unshaven, on the sitting-room sofa, when she came in alone and sat down beside him. She looked intently at him, her green eyes dilated, and he could smell the rain on her woolen dress. When she spoke, her voice sounded strained, and he felt at once an overwhelming sense of relief.

"Couldn't you have telephoned me or come to see me?"

"I haven't got a telephone or a car," he said cheerfully, and tried to take her hand. She withdrew it sharply.

"I've been waiting five days," she said. "Five days waiting around for a man who's grubby, unshaven, and who spends his time doing crossword puzzles."

She was clearly beside herself with rage, and Gilles was overjoyed, more so than he would have thought possible. Strangely enough, for once, he did not feel that he had brought off a clever maneuver, but simply that he had been mistaken about her. He tried to justify himself.

"I wasn't sure you wanted to see me."

"I told you I loved you," she said sullenly. "Didn't I, yes or no?"

She got up and went toward the door, so quickly that he was taken by surprise. She was already in the hall, putting on her raincoat, by the time he caught up with her. Odile, or the cook, might arrive at any second, but he took her in his arms anyway. The sound of the rain outside, the anger of the woman in his arms, the unexpectedness of her visit, the smell of wood coming from the stairs, the silence of the house—all this had a slightly intoxicating effect on Gilles. He kissed her gently, but she kept her head obstinately lowered until finally, with calm deliberation, she raised it and put her arms around his neck. He led her to his room without the slightest subterfuge, with the careless audacity—and moreover the luck—that desire engenders, and they became real lovers at last, only as two people can who are in love with love—and know it. It was thus that Gilles rediscovered his taste for pleasure.

Night was falling. Gilles could hear his sister downstairs, giving orders in a voice that seemed louder than usual. Suddenly, he realized why, and turning towards Nathalie he began to laugh silently. She opened her eyes lazily, and closed them again at once.

"Where did you leave your car?"

"At the front door. Why? Oh, my God, I completely forgot about your sister and Florent. I only meant to tell you what I thought of you and then go. What will they think?"

Her voice was languid, calm, the voice of a woman after the act of love, and Gilles wondered how he could have survived for nearly four months without hearing that special voice in his ear. He smiled.

"What do you suppose they'll think?"

She turned over without answering.

"I knew it," she said. "I knew it would be like this, you and me. I knew it from the first moment I saw you. It's funny."

"It's better than funny," he said. "Come on, let's go and have an eggnog."

"You mean go down just like that, with no explanation?"

"It's the only way," Gilles said. "Don't ever explain. Get dressed."

There was a renewed authority and decisiveness in his tone, which had been absent for a long time, and he suddenly became aware of it on seeing the cheerfully ironic smile which Nathalie gave him from the pillow. He leaned over and kissed her shoulder.

"Yes," he said, "how pitiful we are—suddenly carried away by something beyond our control. Nathalie, how can I thank you?"

They made their entrance into the little sitting room with the light-heartedness that seems to manifest itself in people over thirty when they have successfully accomplished such a weighty enterprise as love-making, and it was Odile and

59

Florent who jumped to their feet, blushing. "What a surprise!" Florent exclaimed, raising his arms to heaven, while Odile congratulated Nathalie on her bravery in coming to see them in such weather, when she herself had not had the courage to put her nose out of doors. Which signified, of course, that neither of them had noticed the car which had been parked at their doorstep for the past two hours. This joint demonstration of tact and acute myopia delighted Gilles greatly as Odile chatted on about the weather and the need for something to warm them up—at which point she blushed yet again. Florent rushed to get the port bottle. Sitting on the sofa, her long slender hands lying in her lap like inanimate objects, Nathalie smiled and chatted, darting a quick glance from time to time at Gilles, who stood leaning against the mantelpiece with a slightly superior air, amused by this little provincial comedy.

"It looks as though the Cassignacs will have dreadful weather for their open-air dance," Odile remarked with a woebegone look.

"Are you going?" asked Nathalie.

"I was afraid that Gilles wouldn't want to go," said Odile unthinkingly, "but now . . ."

She stopped short, horror-stricken, and Florent, who was about to hand her a glass, froze in his tracks, rolling his eyes furiously. Gilles almost burst out laughing and quickly turned away.

". . . but now that he's looking a little better," Odile went on half-heartedly, "perhaps he'd like to come with us."

She looked imploringly at her brother, who reassured her with a nod. Nathalie's eyes were brimming with tears; evidently she, too, was having difficulty suppressing wild laughter. "My God," Gilles thought suddenly, "what do I not owe this woman. How long is it since I've felt this lassitude, this beautiful after-love when you're equally vulnerable to laughter or tears?"

"Of course I'll go," he said gaily. "But I won't dance with anyone except you two."

He smiled at Nathalie with such tenderness that she lowered her eyelids and looked away.

"I must go home," she said. "I'll see you tomorrow, then, at the Cassignacs'?"

Gilles helped her into her coat. He opened the door of her car for her and put his head through the window.

"What about tomorrow afternoon?"

"I can't," she said despairingly, "I've got a Red Cross Committee meeting."

He roared with laughter.

"Of course, you're the wife of an important official."

"Don't laugh," she said hurriedly, in a low, trembling voice, "don't laugh. You mustn't laugh."

She let in the clutch, leaving Gilles nonplussed and somewhat pensive. All that evening, his sister lavished unusual little attentions on him, much to his amusement. Women love to see their brothers, even their sons, transformed into lovers, especially when, like Odile, their own lives are entirely devoid of romance. It is their way of avenging an obscure sense of defeat.

11

The weather turned out fine for the Cassignacs, and the garden party was in full swing when they arrived. It was the beginning of June, deliciously mild on the big terrace, and the bright dresses of the women, the laughter of the men, the scent of the chestnut trees gave Gilles an immediate impression of the unreality of prewar days. There was something relaxed in the relations between these people, a sort of tenderness in the atmosphere, that made him see Paris, the Paris he had loved so much, as a nightmare. Odile was holding him by the arm, introducing him right and left as they waited to find their hostess in the crowd. Suddenly he felt her hand tighten on his arm and she stopped in front of a tall, rather handsome man who looked curiously English among these people from the Southwest.

"François, have you met my brother? Gilles, this is Monsieur Silvener."

"But of course, we dined together at the Rouargues'," said Silvener in surprise.

"That's right," said Gilles, who hadn't the slightest recollection of him. "So this is her husband," he thought. "Not bad. Very rich, so they say. Not very relaxed. Or very amusing. Does she whisper the same things to both of us? I doubt it." And as he shook hands with Silvener, he longed to hold Nathalie in his arms again.

"Do you live in Paris?" asked Silvener.

"Yes, for the past ten years. Do you go there often?"

"As little as possible. My wife loves it, of course, but personally I find it gets on my nerves very quickly."

Odile, as though relieved to see that Silvener and Gilles had not immediately challenged one another to a duel, moved off to another group. Gilles would have liked to follow her: he had always hated being friendly with the husbands or ex-lovers of his mistresses, out of a last vestige of moral or aesthetic scruple. But Silvener was alone and it was difficult for him to leave him. He looked around for Nathalie, in vain, while making conversation about the Paris traffic problem, hotel rates, and the infernal din of big cities. "I'm leaving," he thought, suddenly fed up, "I've had enough of this. She could at least have been on the lookout for me." He was trying to think of some polite phrase with which to get away from Silvener when she came up to them. She was wearing a green dress, very well cut, which matched her eyes. She looked at him, smiling, and in that very instant, Gilles decided to stay.

"You know one another, I believe," Silvener said.

"We met at the Rouargues'," Gilles repeated with a bow, pleased because the phrase was both true and free of double meaning—another thing he hated between clandestine lovers. Nathalie smiled.

"So we did. Monsieur Lantier, Madame Cassignac, who's

crippled, spotted you from her wheelchair and sent me to bring you over to her. Will you come?"

Gilles followed her, nodding vaguely on the way to people he thought he recognized, and smiling at the thought of the expression on Jean's face if he had seen him there.

They had crossed the terrace and were making their way towards a shady garden where their hostess was enthroned in her wheelchair beneath a rusty wrought-iron pergola, when Nathalie swerved to the right like a shying horse and pulled him behind a tree. Instantly he felt her hair against his cheek, her body against his, and the rashness, the folly of her action filled him with such passionate warmth that he began to cover her with kisses, as though he were madly in love with her.

"Stop," she said, "stop. Oh Gilles, stop, I . . ."

There were people coming down the path and he just had time to bend down and retie an imaginary shoelace, while Nathalie, with an abstracted air, shook her hair back into place. She exchanged light-hearted greetings with the passersby, and introduced Gilles. Then, with his heart still beating hard, he went and kissed the hand of the elderly Madame Cassignac, who congratulated him on his articles, which she had obviously never read. After which, decorously this time, they went back to the terrace. Dusk was falling, Madame Cassignac's grandson had put some rock records on an ancient record player, and the very young were rhythmically swaying their hips beneath the indulgent and ironic gaze of a few grownups in varying stages of decrepitude. Gilles was annoyed with himself for having let his feelings run away with him.

"You know, your husband's not at all bad," he said, in a tone of appreciation that was almost insulting.

She looked at him.

"Don't talk to me about him. Let's not talk about him."

"I'm only trying to be objective," said Gilles in the same joking manner.

"I'm not asking you to be objective," she said curtly, and left him. He lit a cigarette, began to laugh, and suddenly was overcome with self-disgust. Who did he think he was? Why was he putting on this act of the sophisticated, cynical, detached Parisian on holiday? Where had he picked up this cheap stereotype of the seducer? He leaned against a tree for a moment. He must go away, disappear, leave this woman to her life. She was too good for him, too genuine for the miserable, degenerate poseur he had become. He must tell her so, at once.

But when he found her, she was not alone. His unhappy victim was surrounded by three men who were laughing uproariously; one of them was extremely good-looking and all were visibly fascinated by her. Gilles asked her to dance, but the handsome stranger gently restrained him.

"You're not going to take Nathalie away from her bodyguards, because we three are her bodyguards! My name is Pierre Lacour, this is Jean Noble, and this is Pierre Grandet. Join us in a drink and tell us about Paris."

His eyes gleamed with mischief and self-assurance, as did those of his two friends, and even Nathalie's. Gilles felt ridiculous. This fellow must be her lover too, or else had been, and he was being patronizing to the little Parisian who gave himself such airs. To think that he had been worried about making her unhappy, to think that he had had scruples! He smiled, and helped himself to a whiskey.

"Nathalie was in fact ripping apart a book which I reviewed favorably," said the one called Lacour. "You see, I teach literature at Limoges University, and from time to time I offer a modest contribution to the local paper."

"So we're colleagues," said Gilles politely. Inwardly he was raging. What a fool he had been! How could he have thought that a woman who had thrown herself at his head, who had given herself to him just about the first time he had asked her, who was so expert at love-making, could have fallen in love with him? She was a nymphomaniac, and a cultured one too. He was surprised at his own fury. It was a long time since he had been so angry.

"May I insist on this dance?" he said. "For once they've put on something slow, and I'm too old for those acrobatics."

Nathalie smiled, put her hand on his arm, and they moved to the small, circular dance floor which had been laid on the terrace. They danced a few steps in silence, then Nathalie looked up at him.

"You're not going to start on that again?"

"On what?"

"François."

He had quite forgotten the incident. No, that wasn't it at all. . . . He gave her an affectionate smile.

"No, I won't start on that again. I say, he's rather charming, your number-one bodyguard, the professor of literature. He seems to adore you."

Her reply made him miss a step.

"I should hope so. He's my brother. He's good-looking, isn't he?

"Don't hold me so close, Gilles, everyone's looking at us. Gilles, Gilles, are you happy?"

"Yes," he said.

And, at that moment, it was absolutely true.

12

He had received a telegram from Jean that morning urgently asking him to telephone, and by midday he was suffocating from the heat in the tiny post office in Bellac, at once anxious and thrilled by this call which revived his sense of professional importance. He had to run the gauntlet of three affectionate secretaries before Jean came on the line, his voice suddenly very remote, as though coming from another planet.

"Hello, Gilles? Are you better? Good. I knew you would be. I'm delighted, old man."

"Poor fool," thought Gilles unkindly. "You didn't know anything of the sort. You couldn't possibly have known. Don't tell me you share Odile's faith in the air of the Limousin. The reason why I'm better is because there's a woman here who loves me and whose love I can tolerate. How could you have foreseen that?"

Nevertheless, he replied briefly and calmly, like a badly wounded man who is off the danger list at last and realizes what a scare he has given his friends.

"You see," Jean was saying, "Lenoux has had this appalling row with the boss. The idea is that you should take over the whole foreign desk. It's true, I promise you. The suggestion didn't even come from me. What do you say?"

He sounded overjoyed, and Gilles tried in vain to respond. The idea left him cold. The job he had wanted so badly now seemed completely unreal.

"Mind you, it won't be before September. I told the boss quite simply that you were off on a jaunt somewhere. It wasn't the moment to mention your depression—it would have put him off. . . . You ought to come back at once, for a day or two at least, so that he can see you. . . . You know what our little pals are like. . . ."

"So my depression would have put him off," thought Gilles sardonically. "A serious man hasn't the right to be under the weather. A good journalist must be happy, active, even lecherous—anything except depressed. My God, soon they'll start poisoning unhappy people. . . . They'll have quite a job."

"Are you pleased?" asked Jean's voice, full of genuine affection. "When can you get here?"

"I'll take the train tomorrow," said Gilles without conviction. "There isn't a plane, you see. I'll be arriving about eleven in the evening."

"Why can't you take it today?"

Gilles felt a sudden irritation.

"What's the rush? If he's really decided to take me on, he can wait one more day!"

There was a silence, followed by Jean's voice, rather curt and disappointed.

68

"I just thought there was a rush from your point of view. I'll meet your train tomorrow. Good-by, old boy."

He hung up, and Gilles wiped his forehead in the overheated kiosk. He was meeting Nathalie at three. Was that what had held him back? It was true, and he knew it, that there *was* a rush, as there always was on the paper when an important job fell vacant. In fact it must be causing quite a stir. And he, because of a woman, might quite possibly miss his chance. He nearly rang Jean back, to tell him he would come immediately. He wavered, stammering, in front of the postmistress. Then, through the window, he caught a glimpse of the lush countryside, the corn waving in the wind, and he thought of Nathalie's body, her warmth, her intelligence, and rushed out. Florent was waiting for him at the wheel of his car.

"Well, was it good news?"

He looked genuinely worried and Gilles, who hardly ever "saw" him, had a moment of real affection for those big blue eyes. He smiled, not without a certain effort, as Florent just scraped past a truck.

"I've been offered a rather important job on the paper."

"Everything's working out," exclaimed Florent, "everything's working together. It's what I've always said: life's like the waves of the ocean, first a bad one, then a good one, and so on. . . ."

He made wavelike gestures with his hands, threatening to send them into the ditch. He might be right, at that. But Gilles dared not tell him he was as afraid of the good waves as of the bad ones, as afraid of his new responsibilities and Nathalie's passion as of mediocrity and loneliness.

13

"So you're leaving tomorrow," she repeated.

She was lying fully dressed on Gilles's bed, a thoughtful expression on her face. He had told her everything as soon as she arrived, not entirely displeased to be playing the part of the successful career man, a role which made a pleasant change from that of the neurotic. He had even been carried away to the point of giving her an almost lyrical description of the importance of his new job, the moral responsibility to their readers which it entailed, the absorbing interest of foreign affairs; in short, he had been seized with the enthusiasm in front of her he should have shown over the telephone to Jean. Perhaps, he told himself sardonically, it was remorse at having disappointed Jean that drove him to dazzle his mistress in this way. She seemed anything but dazzled, however. Simply rather blank.

"I shall be away for a week, perhaps two. Then I'll be

back. I don't start until autumn, you know."

"Like schoolchildren," she said absently.

He felt rather annoyed. He had talked himself into believing in the importance and interest of the job, and he was now angry with himself, angry with her, because he had risked losing it for the sake of an afternoon with her. All the same, he did not dare say so to her. It was she who brought it up.

"If it's so important, why didn't you take the train this afternoon?"

"Because we'd arranged to meet."

Although this was quite true, he felt his words rang false. She looked him in the eyes.

"Perhaps you simply felt one can't leave a woman with a scribbled note even if one has only known her for a fortnight?"

She spoke calmly and he found himself shaking his head, almost blushing, like someone caught in a lie. Perhaps she was right, after all, perhaps he would never come back. Paris would take him back to its bosom—Paris, the summer, his friends, the sea, travel. Perhaps she had never been more than a fortnight's interlude in early summer in the Limousin. Suddenly, through the eyes of this woman, he saw himself free, self-confident, once more as light-hearted and invulnerable as he had been all his life. A wave of tenderness swept over him; he did not know whether it was gratitude at having rediscovered this gay, lost image of himself, or simply anticipatory pity in case he did not return. He leaned toward her.

"What would you do if I didn't come back?"

"I'd come and get you," she said. "Kiss me."

He kissed her, instantly forgetting both Paris and politics.

71

At first he thought, coarsely, that whatever happened he would miss her as a lover, then that too was forgotten and he remained for a long time motionless, his head on her shoulder, terrified at the idea of leaving her even for a week. She stroked his head and the nape of his neck, without saying a word. The glow of the setting sun filled the room, and it suddenly struck him that this was a moment he would never forget. Whatever happened.

"I'll take you to the station tomorrow," she said. "To Vierzon, not Limoges. And I'll come and meet you when you get back."

There was a strange, almost despairing calm in her voice.

PART THREE

Paris

14

It was only when he saw her running along the station platform to meet him that he remembered Eloise. Jean was walking along behind, looking amiably tactful, and Gilles found himself with his lips glued to the mouth of this stranger, utterly aghast at his own forgetfulness. "It's true," he told himself, "she exists and she lives with me, it's terrifying. . . . Jean might have warned me." He laughed to himself at this ingenuous idea. As if your friends were supposed to remind you that you had a resident mistress every time you returned from a vacation. . . . At the same time, Eloise's scent and the touch of her lips faintly disgusted him. He remembered Nathalie's last kiss at Vierzon three hours earlier, the note of breathlessness, of desperation, in their farewell, and he was filled with irrational anxiety. What if she had had an accident on the way back along the twisting road, her eyes filled with the tears he had suddenly noticed at the last minute? He himself had sat dazed in his compartment for at least five minutes before pulling himself together and making firmly for the bar. He would have been quite incapable of driving at that moment, and she always drove so fast. Very well, but very fast . . . He was becoming idiotic. He detached himself gently from Eloise, clapped Jean on the back, and tried to smile. The station was black with soot, deafening. It was only in Jean's car that he recognized the Paris he loved, blue and languid in the night, his summer Paris. And his heart tightened at the memory of all the happiness he had known in this city during the past ten years, as though it were lost to him forever. He was frightened; once again he felt lost and helpless. He would have given anything to be lying in a field in the Limousin in the shelter of Nathalie's arms.

"Glad to be back?" asked Jean.

"Very. How have you been?"

He was doing his best to appear cheerful and friendly.

"It's lucky Jean told me you were coming," said Eloise's voice from the back, gaily enough. "You didn't exactly bombard me with news."

"I wanted to save Eloise the trouble of coming to meet you by taxi," said Jean, "so I dropped by to pick her up. She was flabbergasted."

He too was laughing, but his gaiety was somewhat forced. He gave Gilles a sidelong glance, as though to make sure he hadn't put his foot in it.

"I did try and ring you," lied Gilles, "but there was never any answer."

"I'm not surprised," said Eloise, "I've been modeling all day. And guess who for? For *Vogue!*"

She sounded jubilant. "Well, thank God for that,"

thought Gilles cynically, "at least something's gone right." But one thought was now uppermost in his mind: to telephone Nathalie or get Jean to do it. They had agreed that he was not to telephone her until the following day because of the risk, at eleven o'clock at night, of her husband answering, but he could not shake off this stupid obsession about accidents. Of course he wasn't in love with her, but he nevertheless wanted, for his own peace of mind, to know that she was alive. On the other hand, how could he telephone from his flat with Eloise clinging to his side and Jean wanting to talk shop?

"You look much better," said Jean. "You've even got a bit of a tan. That's just as well, since I told the boss that you were on the Côte d'Azur with an Italian starlet."

"What I have to put up with!" said Eloise with a giggle, and Gilles sank deeper into his seat, embarrassed. But he could not suppress a twinge of pride at the idea of Nathalie as an Italian starlet: not only was she more beautiful, but she had qualities not usually found in Italian starlets.

His flat was unchanged, if somewhat more feminine. An enormous teddy bear, a gift to Eloise from some photographer, made him shudder momentarily, but he quickly looked away. He felt totally indifferent, a complete stranger in his own home. He sat down in an armchair in the hope that Jean and Eloise would follow suit and allow him to wander, as it were absent-mindedly, into the bedroom in order to get to the telephone. But Eloise, like a good housewife, had already dragged his suitcase into the bedroom and was noisily opening closet doors. More and more exasperated, he was not listening to Jean, who, noticing this at last, stopped talking and looked at him questioningly. Gilles stood up.

"Excuse me a minute, old man. I promised I'd telephone my sister as soon as I arrived—she's as fussy as an old hen, and you see . . ."

He was jabbering. Jean merely nodded and smiled politely. Gilles couldn't help returning his smile, and a wave of affection for his old comrade in arms came over him. He gave him a pat on the head on his way into the bedroom, where he nonchalantly picked up the telephone, sat on the bed, and consulted the directory. He needed to dial a dozen digits to get Nathalie.

"Who are you calling at this hour of the night?" asked Eloise, putting his blue jacket on a hanger.

"My sister," he answered laconically.

He dialed the number. If her husband answered, he would hang up. There were several long rings and then, very close and very wide-awake, Nathalie's voice. He noticed that the hand with which he was holding the receiver was moist.

"Hello," he said, "it's me. I wanted to let you know I've arrived safely. And I just wanted to know if you got back all right."

He spoke very fast, in a deliberately casual tone of voice. There was a silence, followed by Nathalie's voice, troubled and a little husky.

"I think you must have the wrong number," she said.

Then, a second later:

"Not at all, you haven't disturbed me in the least," she said almost tenderly, and rang off. Gilles waited a moment, then said, "Love to you both," into the dead instrument for Eloise's benefit and put down the receiver. He was sweating prodigiously.

So her husband must have been there, beside her, and

she hadn't been able to speak to him. But how quick-witted she was. . . . How comic and endearing that, "You haven't disturbed me in the least," had sounded. And she was alive, of course. And she loved him. Odd, these fits of nerves he got from time to time. . . . He went back to the sitting room, once more the man about town, relaxed, light-hearted, giving no more thought to Nathalie than to Eloise, now that he was reassured about her. It did not occur to him for an instant that if he felt reassured it was because he had needed reassurance.

"It's just like old times," said Eloise's voice in the darkness. "I knew we'd be together for a long time, you and I. A very long time."

Gilles did not reply. He turned over in the bed, furious with himself. He had drunk too much that evening with Jean, they had all three drunk too much, celebrating his return and his new-found glory. When Jean had left around three in the morning, Gilles, instead of feeling sleepy, had felt lively, jubilant, self-confident, in fact a little drunk, and he had made love to Eloise, almost mechanically, as a final demonstration of his power and as he would have done with any woman who happened to be in his bed. In short, he had been unfaithful not only to Nathalie, which hardly mattered since she would never know, but also to himself since, in his drunkenness, he had got only a tense, exacerbated pleasure out of it. Unfaithful in a sense to Eloise, too, who had seen in it a proof of love. He would have to explain things to her, tell her about Nathalie, just when she was beginning to believe again, by his own doing, that he still cared for her. He switched on the light abruptly, reached for a cigarette, registered in a detached way that Eloise was ravishing with her hair spread over the pillow like that, and tried to think of a way to begin. His head ached, he was dog-tired and thirsty.

"It's funny," said Eloise dreamily, "how everything's working out right at the same time. I've got a regular modeling job for *Vogue* thanks to this American photographer, you've got the job you've always dreamed of, and you're better. A month ago I would never have believed it. You did frighten me, you know. Very much. Very, very, very much."

She always talked in this childish way after making love, and Gilles had found it successively endearing and irritating. Now it only redoubled his remorse.

"It's not quite so simple as that," he said in a hoarse voice. "You see, I'm not completely well. I'm going back to my sister's as soon as I've settled this business."

"Well, what with the collections, I'll be working all summer anyhow," she said. "But I'll come and see you between shows. One can fly to Limoges nowadays by Air-Inter."

"That's all it needed," thought Gilles. Now progress was taking a hand in it. He really would have to tell her, in spite of his almost neurotic dread of partings. . . . But not tonight, no, not tonight. He looked at Eloise for the first time since his return, looked at her trusting eyes, her familiar body, all that beauty and tenderness so useless to him now, and he was suddenly filled with such pity for her, for himself, for Nathalie, for love itself, for all the loves destined to end one day in sorrow and regrets, that he fell back on his pillow with tears in his eyes. Eloise leaned toward him.

"Are you sad? Why, just when everything's going so well?"

He switched off the light without answering. Lying with his head resting on his arms, he remembered the meadow by the river's edge and Nathalie's approach. He could smell the warm grass, could see the poplars softly swaying above him, and the strange promise in Nathalie's clear eyes.

15

Fairmont, the editor of the newspaper, was a tall, lean, clumsy man, a hard worker. Scion of a distinguished upper middle-class family, he had astonished everybody by starting a left wing newspaper with his own money, a newspaper which was as genuinely left wing as it was possible to be during that confused period. Nevertheless, he retained certain authoritarian characteristics and it was well known on the paper that, although condemning privilege in all its forms, for several years he had been trying to revive the title of Count de Fairmont for himself, which had lapsed under Charles X. Gilles was in his office, with Jean, trying to show some interest in a ponderous lecture about his future responsibilities.

"Obviously, you'll have to give up your escapades," Fairmont was saying. "I don't want to have to look for you in Saint-Tropez if the Americans make peace in Vietnam. You're very young for the job, I know, and that is all the more reason why you should get down to it seriously. You realize, of course, that it would have gone to Garnier if it hadn't been for this scandal."

Gilles pricked up his ears and looked at Jean, who shook his head, embarrassed.

"I'm out of touch," he said. "It's true, Garnier's been here a long time, he's extremely able. . . ."

"Garnier has been involved in a very unfortunate incident. He's in trouble with the police over a young boy."

"But what has that got to do with the job!" said Gilles.

He was furiously indignant. Jean threw him a placatory glance, but there was no stopping him.

"If I understand you correctly, I owe this job to my sexual inclinations?"

Fairmont gave him an icy stare.

"Not to *your* inclinations, but mine. I don't want to employ an important editor who could be blackmailed. You'll start in September."

Back in Jean's office, Gilles's fury exploded. He paced up and down, gesticulating, while Jean looked on impassively.

"I can't take this job, it's sheer robbery. What difference does that business make? Who does this puritan think he is? How can people be blackmailed for their morals in this day and age? No, I can't accept it. . . . What do *you* think? You might have told me about it! It's true, I'd completely forgotten Garnier."

"You'd forgotten Garnier, and Eloise, and me," said Jean peaceably. "In any case, you needn't worry. If you refuse they'll find someone else. Your friend Thomas, for instance."

"I could care less whether it's Thomas or anyone else. I just can't do this to Garnier myself. He's at least as qualified as I am."

He was chain smoking furiously as he walked round and round the room. Finally Jean stopped him.

"Sit down, you're making me dizzy. I've already talked it over with Garnier. He thinks you're the best choice. He has no illusions whatever about himself. Why not go and see him?"

"That's great!" groaned Gilles. "That's just great!"

He collapsed into an armchair. Jean grinned.

"You're angry because you weren't chosen just for your great brains, aren't you?"

"You don't understand," said Gilles. "It's an injustice, and I dislike being the one who profits from it."

All the same, he was angry. Angry and disgusted. He longed to be rid of it all: Paris and its intrigues, its ukases, its hypocrisies. He longed to be back in the country and the drawing rooms of Limoges, fragile, unassuming, and blue, like his brother-in-law's eyes. He would telephone Nathalie and ask her advice. She would know what to do. There was something naturally pure and uncompromising about her. Something he badly needed.

"I'm going to telephone," he muttered mechanically.

"Who?"

Jean's precisely probing voice surprised him; he was usually the soul of discretion.

"Why do you ask?"

"Because I'm interested. You left like a convict, dragging your chains with you, and you come back treading on air. I'd like to know who's responsible."

"You're quite wrong," Gilles protested, genuinely horrified. "I'm not in the least in love with her," he added naïvely, "I hardly know her. She's been sweet to me, that's all."

Jean began to laugh.

"That's all? And yet when I tell you about the job of a lifetime you don't turn up until the following day. And you're astounded at the sight of Eloise. And you go to extraordinary lengths to telephone this woman as soon as you arrive. And at the slightest provocation you want to ask her advice. Otherwise that's all. Don't stare at me as though you'd never seen me, you look frightfully stupid."

"That really is the limit," said Gilles. (And he stammered with rage in his desire to be believed and to believe himself.) "I tell you I'm fond of her, that's all. I suppose you know my own feelings better than I do?"

"Not only now," said Jean, "but for the past fifteen years. Come on, we'll go and have a drink and you can tell me all about her."

They went to the Sloop and sat down on the terrace. The weather was deliciously mild, the sun warming their faces, and Gilles treated Jean to a sober and precise account of his provincial affair. To his own surprise, he had the greatest difficulty in introducing the note of cynicism or irony which would have convinced Jean of his good—or rather, bad—faith. But he tried his hardest. Jean puffed at his pipe, apparently half-asleep.

"If that's all it is," he said, "why are you going back there? Go south with Eloise, as usual."

"That's not the point!" said Gilles, exasperated. "I'm not saying this woman doesn't interest me. Psychologically . . ."

"You've been talking about her for three-quarters of an hour," Jean said. "I've timed you. And you haven't even drunk your beer, in spite of the sun and your own eloquence. Poor Eloise. And poor François. Yes, the husband. Now I even know his name."

Gilles looked at him, aghast. He felt a momentary dizziness, a feeling of something welling up inside him, filling him with warmth and terror and relief all at the same time. He reached out his hand, picked up his glass, and brought it ceremoniously to his lips. Then he threw back his head with his eyes closed, and the tepid beer filled his mouth and throat, and he had the feeling he could swallow pint after pint of it, that he would always, forever, be as deliciously thirsty as this. He put down his glass.

"You're right," he said. "I must be in love with her."

"I'm some use to you after all," said Jean, unsmiling.

16

He spent the day in a dream. He longed to telephone
Nathalie, to declare his love for her, triumphantly. At the
same time he wanted to take it back to her as a surprise, like
some marvelous and unexpected present, to see her face
when he told her. If he could only wait a few more days, if
he could only wait until he arrived at the station and she
was there to meet him. . . . As soon as they were outside the
town he would make her stop the car and would take her
face between his hands and say to her: "I'm desperately in
love with you, you know." The idea of her happiness filled
him with pride and tenderness, he felt recklessly spend-
thrift. Carried away by his own generosity, he stopped at a
jeweler's and spent his last few francs on a silly little pin,
which softened him even more, so that when he telephoned
her from a nearby café at five o'clock, as agreed, his heart
was overflowing.

She answered at once but in a curt, almost cold voice which at first surprised, then wounded him. "God, that's always the way," he thought instantly to himself. He knew that in love one side always ends up by hurting the other and that sometimes, rarely, this situation can be reversed. But so quickly to be wounded by her when he had only just admitted to himself that he loved her, while she was still unaware of it, seemed to him both unfair and mortifying. At the same time the wound itself instantly confirmed the truth of his love.

"What's the matter?" he asked cheerfully.

"It's been terribly hot here and there have been frightful thunderstorms all day and I'm . . . I'm scared stiff of thunderstorms. Don't laugh," she added quickly, "I can't help it."

He did laugh, though, with a mixture of relief and surprise. It was the first sign of childishness he had observed in her. Her rash, impetuous, wholehearted behavior had until now seemed to him closer to adolescence than to the timorousness of bourgeois childhood.

"I've bought you a present," he said.

"How sweet of you. Listen, Gilles, I must ring off. It's very dangerous to hold an electrical instrument during a thunderstorm. Ring me back tomorrow."

"But there's nothing electric about telephones. They're . . ."

"Please, please!" she said, in a voice that was wild and distorted with fear. "Good-by."

She hung up, leaving him nonplussed, receiver in hand, trying to laugh. Trying to tell himself that the next time there was a thunderstorm over Limoges, he would make love to her and see whether pleasure would prevail over fear. Nevertheless, he felt sad, abandoned; the sun had set over the streets and his present now seemed infinitely more ridiculous than touching. He wanted to see her at once. There was always Air-Inter, the famous Air-Inter, which he could resort to if worse came to worst, if he felt too bad. He telephoned Orly; there was no flight until the next day. The train had left, he had sold his Simca, and he was broke. And he had an appointment next day with the business manager of the paper to discuss his new salary, and he had to talk to Eloise, and life was hell. The truth was that he had been too happy all day; he should have been warned. The idea that he had reached a point where he could think "Everything has to be paid for" filled him with self-disgust. No, he was by no means cured yet! He was now doubly ill, not only depressed, but at the mercy of a stranger. A strange woman who claimed to love him yet hung up on him because of a little thunder. He brooded over his resentment beneath the friendly gaze of the *patronne* of the café until at last, feeling her eyes on him, he tried to smile.

"Isn't it beautiful weather?" he said.

"A bit too hot," the woman said, amiably. "There's going to be a storm." He was quick to seize the opening.

"Are you afraid of thunderstorms?"

She burst out laughing.

"Thunderstorms? You must be joking. No, it's only taxes that frighten me."

She was about to enlarge on this subject, but seeing Gilles's crestfallen look, she went on, with the instinctive kindness and the extraordinary insight such women often develop as a result of long acquaintance with the faces, happy or miserable, of solitary habitués.

"Mind you, my niece, who comes from the Morvan, where they have terrible ones, she's never managed to get used to them. Even in the middle of a meal, if she hears thunder she dives under the bed. It's nerves."

"Yes," said Gilles, delighted, "it's nerves," thinking to himself that Nathalie had so far been a great deal more pre-occupied with *his* nerves than with her own and that it was probably only fair that the reverse should now apply. He launched into a long conversation, standing and being stood several glasses of port—a drink he normally detested but which reminded him of his brother-in-law's cocktails—and left the café slightly fuddled but in a more optimistic frame of mind. First of all he must talk to Eloise. Then tomorrow he would go to the office and try to get an advance, and by tomorrow evening there was no reason why he shouldn't be able to leave. Already he could imagine the seventy-mile drive with Nathalie, seventy enchanted miles through the night, seventy miles of love talk. Why had he spoken to her of a week or two of separation? As a defense, no doubt, in order to persuade himself, by persuading her, that a week without her was possible, or bearable, and also to persuade himself of the reality of Paris, ambition, friends—a hopeless idea now, since for the last two days everything had been unreal, he had seen and felt nothing, only the hills of the Limousin and Nathalie's face existed for him. But what would she think, seeing him back so soon, knowing he was enslaved? Wouldn't she succumb to that fatal sense of security, of slightly bored familiarity one feels with a person one takes for granted? Or would she be overcome with joy? Recalling in rapid succession her tear-filled eyes at the sta-tion and then her curtness on the telephone this afternoon, he understood that she was two different women, and by multiplying, complicating, blending them together, he in-voluntarily prepared himself for a deeper love.

Eloise was watching television when he came in, but she jumped up and flung her arms around his neck. He remembered a similar scene which seemed long ago until he realized to his surprise it had been only a month before. It seemed to him so much had happened since then. But what had in fact happened? He had spent an interminably boring two weeks with his sister and then for the next ten days made love to a woman in the afternoons. Looked at one way, that was all it amounted to. But he no longer wished to look at it that way.

"Well, how did it go? Did you see Fairmont?"

"Yes," he said, "I saw him and everything's settled."

He had no desire to go into the question of Garnier with her. He wanted to talk only to Nathalie about that. Perhaps it was one way of defining love: the desire to tell everything to one person only.

"Have you any port?" he murmured, and immediately regretted his words; he was behaving like a guest.

"Port? But you've always hated the stuff."

"I've just had three and I don't like mixing my drinks, and . . ." (he cleared his throat) "I need a drink."

There, he had taken the first step. She would say, "Why?" and he would reply, "Because I must talk to you." But her mind was on another tack altogether.

"Of course, you poor thing, you've had a terrible day," she exclaimed. "I'll just pop down to the liquor store, I won't be a minute."

"Don't bother," he said miserably, but the door had already slammed behind her. He went to the window and watched her mincing model's walk as she crossed the street and entered the shop. He glanced around the room with a hunted look: there were his favorite cigarettes on the coffee table, his evening paper neatly folded, and a vase of fresh flowers. He knew without looking that his white shirt and his gray suit, the lightweight one, were laid out on the bed in the next room. Even the teddy bear, the frightful teddy bear about which he hadn't said a word to her, had disappeared. She must have put his silence down to kindness on his part, when in fact it was only attributable to complete indifference. And he, like a drunken, thoughtless cad, had made love to her. He hated himself. He would tell all this to Nathalie too; he would hide nothing from her. Priding himself in advance on his honesty and self-abasement, it did not occur to him to wonder to what extent he was anxious to reduce his shame by confessing it, and thus give his break with Eloise more weight in Nathalie's eyes.

As he gloomily drank his port, he decided to talk to Eloise after the television news. But she was longing to watch the next program, a serial which she had been following with passionate interest for the past month, as had his sister, Odile. He was thus the unwilling beneficiary of fifty minutes' reprieve, which served only to increase his discomfiture. He was tempted to take her off somewhere else, to the Club, for example, and to explain everything to her there, surrounded by music and people; it would make things easier. But that was too cowardly.

"Aren't you hungry?" she asked, turning off the set.

"No. Eloise . . . I've been wanting to tell you . . . I . . . I met someone else, in the country, and I . . . I . . ."

He was stammering dreadfully. Eloise stood stock-still, her face pale, staring at him.

"She helped me a lot," he went on hurriedly. "In fact, it's thanks to her that I'm back on my feet. I want to say how sorry I am, about this and about last night. I shouldn't have done that."

Eloise sat down again slowly. She said nothing.

"I'm going back there. Naturally, you must stay here as long as you like. You know that you and I are friends for life."

("How inane and clumsy can you get?" he thought to himself. "It's the classic breakup, in all its banality and cruelty. But there's nothing else I can say.")

"Are you in love with her?" asked Eloise. She seemed incredulous.

"Yes. At least, I think so. And she loves me," he added quickly.

"In that case, why . . . why last night?"

She did not even look at him. She was not crying, but just staring at the television screen as though some invisible film were being shown there for her alone.

"I . . . I wanted you, I suppose," he said. "Please forgive me. I should have told you everything right away."

"Yes," she said, "you should have."

That was all. Now the silence was becoming unbearable. Why couldn't she shout, ask questions, do something outrageous which would give him a chance to breathe! He ran his hands through his hair; he was drenched with sweat. She still said nothing. He stood up and walked across the room.

"Do you want a drink?"

She raised her head. She was crying, and instinctively he went towards her, but she drew back from him, her hand in front of her eyes.

"Go away," she said. "Please, Gilles, go away at once . . . I'll leave in the morning. No, please, go away."

He rushed down the stairs and out into the street, his

heart thumping. He went on running until, gasping for breath, he leaned against a tree and put his arms around the trunk. He was half-dead with shame and misery.

"I'm glad it's you," Garnier was saying.

They were in the bar of the Hotel Pont-Royal, an underground bar where, winter and summer, the light never changed. Gilles had slept in the hotel; he was unshaven, his shirt was dirty, and he had had nightmares. Oddly enough it was Garnier, a big, powerful man with gray hair, gray eyes, and an expression of great sweetness, who seemed the more at ease.

"This . . . the job should have been yours," said Gilles. "I don't like taking it from you."

"It's not your fault. Fairmont doesn't like my wicked ways, that's all."

He laughed, and Gilles blushed.

"Listen," Garnier went on gently, "it isn't as bad as all that. 'All is lost save honor.' I really love this boy. The fact that he told me he was nineteen when in fact he's only seventeen, and that when they picked him up he eventually told them what he lived on, or rather whom—all that's quite natural. I could easily have denied it. They had no proof. But that's where I would have sacrificed my honor—denying him in order to save my own reputation. Comic, isn't it?"

"What will you do?" asked Gilles.

"He'll be out in six months. He'll be eighteen then. And he'll be free to decide whether to see me or not."

Gilles looked at him with admiration.

"But if he doesn't come back to you," he said, "you'll have lost everything for nothing. . . ."

"I've never lost anything I've given," said Garnier calmly.

"It's what you steal from people that you pay dearly for, my dear boy, remember that."

He chuckled.

"You must think I'm an odd one to be such a moralizer. But believe me, the day you're ashamed of what you love, you're finished. Finished with yourself too. Now let's talk shop."

He gave Gilles various tips to which he hardly listened. He was thinking about what he had stolen from Eloise, he was thinking that he would never be ashamed of Nathalie, he was thinking that he would love her as tenderly, as honorably, as Garnier loved his young man. He would tell her all this; he would talk to her about Garnier; he longed to see her again. In half an hour's time he would go round to the office, settle the money question as quickly as possible, lunch with Jean, ask him to look after Eloise, pack his bags, and catch the five o'clock train. He would telephone Limoges here and now.

Nathalie's voice sounded gay and loving, and he was suddenly overwhelmed with happiness.

"I'm terribly sorry about yesterday," she said at once. "I really was scared. It's nerves."

"I know," he said. "What would you say if I came back tonight?"

There was a silence.

"Tonight?" she said. "No, really, Gilles, it's too good to be true. Can you?"

"Yes, I've had enough of this town. And I miss you," he added restrainedly. "I'm coming by train. Can you meet me at Vierzon?"

"Oh God," she said, dismayed, "we're dining at the Coudercs'! What shall I do?"

The genuine distress in her voice comforted Gilles. He said stoically:

"I'll go all the way to Limoges and take a taxi. I'll see you tomorrow. Can we lunch together? Or do you have the Red Cross?"

"Oh, Gilles," she said, "Gilles, you have no idea . . . lunch with you tomorrow, how wonderful . . . waiting is awful."

"Can you pick me up at my sister's at twelve? And can you let her know I'm coming?"

He suddenly felt organized, decisive, virile. He was putting the chaos and confusion of Paris behind him. He was coming alive again.

"I'll drop by there later," she said. "And I'll be there tomorrow at twelve. Everything all right with you?"

"There were a few complications, quite a few, but I . . . I've sorted it all out," he ended firmly.

"That was putting it mildly," he thought. "I've taken someone else's job and I've made a woman miserable." But he couldn't suppress the euphoria he felt or the cruel, incurably clear conscience happiness confers.

"See you tomorrow. I love you."

There was no temptation to say "Me too." She had hung up.

PART FOUR

Limoges

17

The train crawled interminably through the French countryside. To begin with, after leaving the station, there had been the endless sprawling suburbs, almost poetic in the late-afternoon sunlight. Then the first meadows before the Loire, all that lush, shining green, bordered by the immensely elongated shadows of trees, and then the Loire itself, already gray in the twilight. Then night had fallen, and Gilles had turned away from the window and gazed at the placid faces of his traveling companions. He was safe and happy in this train, borne inexorably toward his sister's house, toward Nathalie, toward both peace and love, and it struck him that it was the first time in his life that he had met with this conjunction.

It was after eleven when he reached Limoges. The station was very dark and he was taken completely by surprise when Nathalie suddenly rushed up to him. He dropped his suitcase and took her in his arms without a word, dazed with happiness. They stood there for some time, clinging to one another, swaying in the middle of the station platform, totally oblivious of the lingering stares they attracted. At last he stepped back and looked at her: he had forgotten how enormous, how wide apart, her eyes were.

"How did you manage to get here?"

"I slipped away," she said. "I couldn't bear it any longer. The dinner party was a nightmare. When the soup was served I knew you were at Orléans, during the fish course you were passing through Châteauroux. I thought I was going to faint. Kiss me. Gilles, don't ever go away again."

He kissed her, went with her through the barrier, found her car, threw in his suitcase and himself after it, and took her in his arms.

"You're thinner than ever," she said. "Do you recognize me?"

"I've only been away three days," he said.

"They played bridge after dinner. I said I didn't feel well and was going home. I nearly missed the train, and I almost ran down the entire population of Limoges."

He kissed her. He felt completely happy, completely drained. He had nothing more to say, and yet he remembered that he had an important announcement to make to her: that he loved her, that he had come to realize at last that he loved her. But it no longer seemed nearly as important, as world-shattering, as it had in Paris. Nevertheless, out of a sort of loyalty to the wonderstruck young man he had been for a whole day in Paris, he made the effort:

"You know," he said in a solemn voice which at once sounded ridiculous in his ears, "you know, Nathalie, I love you."

She burst out laughing.

"I should hope so," she said, without the least surprise, "it really would be the last straw if you didn't."

He too began to laugh. She was right; he was an absolute fool. There is no need to formulate such self-evident truths. From the first, she had told him she loved him and she had waited quite calmly until he loved her in his turn. She was a strong-willed woman, or rather a woman whose weaknesses had such strength that he found them irresistible. Well, he had certainly fluffed his big scene, and he was perfectly happy to have done so.

"What news?" she asked.

"I haven't any," he said. "I'm happy. The country was looking very beautiful this evening from the train."

"Funny sort of news . . ."

"Kiss me," he said. "I'll tell you everything tomorrow. We'll go down to the river. Are you still free for lunch?"

"Yes, but I must go home now. François may be back at the house already. I should never have come," she added in a low voice, "it's dreadful to leave you now."

They were passing through Limoges: she was driving slowly and the night air wafted through the window. He held her hand, thinking of nothing, and vaguely realizing that this total absence of thought was what is meant by happiness. She dropped him at a taxi stand and he sat in the same trancelike state during the twenty-mile drive to the old house where he woke up Odile and Florent. Suddenly completely revived, he made them listen, still half-asleep, to the interminable, involved, and comical account of his stay in Paris, which he had spent hours in the train rehearsing for Nathalie's benefit.

He was lying on the riverbank with Nathalie by his side. It was hot, and they squinted their eyes in the last rays of the sun. Nathalie claimed they were getting a sun tan and he ridiculed her, declaring that the only possible tan was a Mediterranean tan and they would hardly even be yellow by the end of summer. At the same time he was perfectly happy as he was, his shirt half-open, his cheek in the cool grass. Everything he had enjoyed so passionately in the past, the relentless sun on the scorching sand, those all too naked and sometimes all too easily available bodies, now filled him with a kind of horror. He needed this soft landscape and this difficult woman. For he could sense that she was annoyed with him. The account he had given her of his stay in Paris had evoked only two reactions in her: an immense compassion for Eloise and an admiring interest in Garnier. Not anything for him. She had shown not a glimmer of jealousy at his confession about the night with Eloise, not a glimmer of sympathy with him over his outrage at Fairmont. She found it all "distressing," a favorite expression of hers. And although it had indeed been his intention to appeal to her sympathy, he had hoped she would console him rather than judge him. But it was clear that she did judge him, and found him weak.

"But after all," he protested, at once irritated and un-concerned (for they had spent the whole afternoon in his bedroom), "after all, what was I supposed to do? Stay with Eloise? Resign from the paper?"

"I don't know. I don't like this sort of predicament. I suspect that that's how you spend your life. Always in the wrong. Without really knowing it. Feeling a bit guilty and rather enjoying it."

"Rotten to the core, eh?" he said with a laugh. "Yes, perhaps."

She was not laughing. He turned over onto his stomach and took her in his arms. She smelled of warm grass. She looked intently at him, her eyes dilated, as though with terror. But he did not see the expression in her eyes; he saw only the blue circles beneath them, for which he was responsible. He smiled, kissing the blue shadows, and said with a laugh:

"Could you love a rotter?"

"One doesn't choose whom one loves."

"For a cultivated woman you're not afraid of platitudes."

"I'm only too afraid of them," she murmured, "they're nearly always true."

He looked at her, saw that she was really afraid, and for a moment shared her fear. Where was it all leading? What if she came to despise him? What if he were really despicable? So much so that she could no longer love him? He buried his head in the grass with a sigh: there was no rest, no peace. He loved this woman and had told her so, and she was afraid of him.

"If you're afraid of me, you should leave me," he murmured.

He felt her cheek, her lips, against the back of his neck.

"I couldn't," she said, "and even if I could, I wouldn't."

"Why not?"

"I've led a very sheltered life, very tame and very boring," she said calmly. "I suppose something like you had to happen to me."

"And do you see it as a stroke of luck or as a catastrophe?"

"As a stroke of luck for the moment," she said.

They lay on the grass without moving, her body leaning lightly against his, and her head resting on his shoulder. He felt a blade of grass tickle his forehead, and he was filled with a sense of utter peace, a kind of torpor. He was almost surprised to hear himself say:

"What do we do about François?"

She drew away from him and lay back on the grass. He had turned his head towards her and could see her profile now, her calm eyes gazing at the sky.

"I don't know," she said. "I shall have to leave him."

He gave a slight start. Unconsciously he had grown used to the ghostly, unobtrusive François. He knew she no longer slept with him; she had told him so and he knew her hatred of compromise too well to doubt her word. But that same integrity could have other consequences.

"What do you intend to do?"

She turned her head towards him and smiled.

"Come and live with you, perhaps, for as long as you go on loving me. After that, I'll see."

She was right, absolutely right: they loved each other, so they ought to live together. He earned more than enough to support a woman. What was this desire for freedom, for solitude, that raged inside him? For all the use he made of his freedom and his solitude, those two joyless bacchantes who had led him straight into a nervous breakdown, he might as well cast them to the four winds. . . . Nevertheless he was afraid. She put out her hand and ruffled his hair.

"Don't worry, Gilles. I won't leave him until the end of summer. And I won't come to you unless you beg me to."

He sat up, suddenly furious. Furious that she had seen through him, furious that there was that sort of thing in him to be seen through.

"I'm not worried in the least. I want you. I want you to come away with me. I want us to leave at once. Talk to him tonight and we'll leave tomorrow."

("But where to?" he was thinking at the same time, "where to? I've only got a few francs left. We can't stay here, after the scandal this will cause. What can we do until September?") She was smiling, and her smile exasperated him.

"I *want* you to come away with me."

He was almost shouting.

"I will," she said calmly. "But only if you ask me to, not if you order me to. Don't shout so, you're all red. Aren't we all right as we are? Where do you want to go?"

"I don't like false situations," he began nobly. . . .

But something in her expression made him falter. She burst out laughing, and he too began to laugh, as he threw himself on her, his hair entangled with hers, kissing her wildly. "Oh, Nathalie, Nathalie," he said, "you know me so well. Oh, how I love you." And she laughed in his arms until the tears ran down her face, her eyes shining, unable to stop.

18

It is strange how a situation made clear-cut by another person's decision becomes comfortable for oneself. Once Nathalie had decided to leave her husband, Gilles no longer felt the slightest embarrassment about François; she was going to leave this other man for him and he felt scarcely involved. From the moment she had broached the idea, pronounced the words, it was no longer a choice to be made but a destiny to be fulfilled. Not for an instant did it occur to him that she might change her mind: like all congenital liars, he was totally credulous. Moreover, he did not feel that he was stealing anything from François: Nathalie's love cries, her sensual ecstasies, were too obviously his, too entirely his doing, for anyone else to claim them. It was not Nathalie the woman he was stealing from François, but Nathalie the "person," that single-minded, uncompromising creature whom, he had to admit, this man had taken very good care of over the years. So much so that he was handing her over to him now as both mistress and mother, at once wanton and severe, everything indeed that Gilles most needed. It was a cynical view, of course, but happiness makes for cynicism. And Gilles was happy.

For one thing, there were the summer afternoons in his room, or rather in a room in the attic, which was more isolated—the former maid's room, which Gilles had reopened and fixed up as best he could. A staircase led up to it from the rear of the house, thus sparing the blushes, not of Nathalie, who did not care in the least, but of Odile who was still troubled by vague qualms. It was a large, dusty, almost empty room in which the bed stood in solitary state except for a red pitch-pine armchair on which Nathalie threw her clothes. Gilles would go up there at about three o'clock, close the shutters, get into bed, open a book, and wait. Soon Nathalie would arrive, get undressed, and slip into bed beside him, sometimes like a primitive creature, without a word, sometimes slowly, indolently, regaling him the while with a comical account of some deathly boring lunch party. He did not know which he preferred, but they always ended up making love, and the heat beneath the roof was such that they would separate streaming with oily sweat, no longer knowing which of them was which, exhausted but never surfeited. He would wipe Nathalie's inert body with the crumpled sheet, rub her down like a pony, while she lay submissively, her eyes closed, her heart still beating furiously beneath his hand. She emerged very slowly from lovemaking, as though from a coma, and he would tease her about it, not without pride. Gradually she came back to life, became aware of something other than the throbbing of her own blood, was able to open her eyes without flinching from the light of the room, feeble though it was, and she would turn her head toward him, as he lay there already smoking a cigarette, with a sort of terrified gratitude.

They talked. Little by little he learned all about her. Her childhood in Tours, her student days in Paris, her first lover, her meeting with François, her marriage. It was a life at once simple and complicated: simple because it contained nothing remotely out of the ordinary, complicated because Nathalie sometimes had a way of falling silent, or of pronouncing an adjective, or even of substituting one clause for another, which made this uneventful and on the whole happy life seem almost heartbreaking. When he asked, "Were you glad to come to Paris to take your degree?" she answered, "Don't be silly . . . it was the first time I had ever been separated from my brother." And over the traditional picture of the young provincial dazzled by Paris and the men she met there, he had to superimpose that of a little girl crying for her brother in a strange town. When he asked her what she had thought of François the first time she met him, she answered, "I felt at once that I could trust him," and it was impossible to get another word out of her. As for her lovers— three, it seemed, before François, and one since—she calmly stated that she had enjoyed making love with them. One day he had foolishly asked her, "As much as with me?" which had provoked a "certainly" that had outraged him. To no avail. She had never loved anyone as she loved him, but she had enjoyed others, and nothing he could do would make her pretend otherwise. This honesty of hers alternatively disarmed and infuriated him, but no subterfuge of his, even in the most passionate moments, could deflect her from it. She would watch him prepare and set his trap and then demolish it with a word and a laugh. And he would join in her laughter. He had never before really laughed at himself with a woman; it was a luxury he had until now indulged in only with Jean or other men, out of some bogus concept of virility. And the opportunity of ridding himself at last of that particular form of vanity bound him closer to her than he realized.

At about six o'clock they would go downstairs and out onto the terrace, where they would find Odile and Florent sitting in their deck chairs, and they would all have an egg-nog and talk about the weather. Odile no longer blushed at the slightest provocation and Florent even indulged in some old-fashioned gallantry, much to Gilles's amusement. Opening wide his big blue eyes, he would ceremoniously offer Nathalie some unspeakable gold-tipped cigarettes which he claimed he alone could find in the district. Nathalie would smoke them stoically under Gilles's sardonic gaze, would sip her eggnog, would say sadly, "It's time I was going," and everyone would protest. The days were growing longer; it was seven o'clock before the cool of the evening came and the shadows of the trees lengthened across the terrace. There were times when Gilles felt himself in the middle of a late nineteenth-century play: the wrought-iron pedestal table, the sweet drinks, the loquacious solicitor . . . then Nathalie would throw back her head, and closing his eyes for a moment he would relive a voluptuous memory of the after-noon. This play, if it was one, was what he wanted more than anything else in the world.

19

There were a great many parties that summer, but Gilles never went to them. He was assumed to be ill, depressed, withdrawn, which suited all concerned—including, he thought, Nathalie. Even though she was ready to go away with him, he still felt very much the lover of a married woman. And who would have suspected this virtuous married woman of driving forty miles every afternoon to jump into bed with a neurotic journalist? When Odile rebuked him for his social remissness, he had only to say something about "running into Silvener" and she would almost apologize, blushing scarlet. Often in the evenings, having watched Florent's little car disappear down the drive on the way to some distant party, leaving him alone in the big house, he would loiter contentedly in the drawing room, occasionally opening a book. Or else he would climb the stairs to the third floor and inhale the odor of Nathalie, of Nathalie's love, on the still unmade bed, and remain there, stretched out, his eyes wide open. Bats flitted noiselessly across the dark-blue sky, the frogs began their monotonous lamentations at the bottom of the garden, a light, scented breeze wafted through the room; and a cool tranquility descended over the heat of their battlefield. He dreamed of Nathalie, not even wishing that she was there. Sometimes he fell asleep in his old sweater, to be awakened by the sound of wheels on the gravel. He would go down, offer a helping hand to Florent who was usually a bit tipsy, and follow them into the kitchen. "What!" Odile would exclaim, "aren't you in bed yet?" But then, delighted to find a more receptive ear than Florent's, she would begin an ecstatic account of the evening which, instead of having been given by the Coudercs, might have been given by the Duchesse de Guermantes. The Royal Highness was invariably Nathalie, whom she always referred to in these recitals as "Madame Silvener," even though she called her by her Christian name every day. Madame Silvener had worn a divine blue dress that evening; Madame Silvener had put the deputy public prosecutor from Brive in his place; the *préfet* had never left Madame Silvener's side, etc., etc. Had he not spent the afternoon naked in bed with her, Gilles would have ended up by developing a schoolboy crush on Madame Silvener. Nevertheless he listened fondly to Odile holding forth, joined with her in mocking the deputy public prosecutor, and tried to imagine the exact blue of the dress. Odile always ended up, probably out of the kindness of her heart, by hinting at some secret melancholy shading the radiant image of Madame Silvener, and Gilles would assume the discreet, abstracted air of the man who knows more than he's prepared to tell. Eventually, awash with romance, Odile would go off to bed with Florent, awash with champagne, these two elements ensuring rapid sleep.

It was two weeks since Gilles had returned from Paris, and not once had he left the house except to accompany Odile to the nearby village to do her morning shopping. His destiny had reached a sort of standstill: it seemed to him that he could spend the rest of his life like this, lounging in the sun, making love to Nathalie in the afternoons, and dreaming away the evenings. It seemed literally absurd to think that in two months' time he would be a political editor, snowed under with work, as jealous of his time as he was prodigal with it now, and that the time would be spent in the gray vortex that was Paris. Indeed, with the easygoingness that had always marred his attitude toward his future, he did not even think about it. On waking up, he would simply wonder whether to go fishing with Florent before lunch, whether Nathalie would be in a tender or demanding mood, whether he could by himself repair the shutter in the hot bedroom. Sometimes, too, on reading the newspaper, he would wonder what on earth could induce one human being to carve up another into eighteen pieces, and would communicate his perplexity to Odile, who screeched like a peacock while Florent, depending on his mood, tapped his forehead with his forefinger or made an imaginary noose with his tie. In short, Gilles was happy; moreover he knew it, and kept repeating it in a dozen different ways to Nathalie with manly pride. "Just think," he said, "just think that two months ago I was an utter wreck, and now I'm a happy man. . . ." There was a sort of smug incredulity in his voice which never failed to amuse Nathalie; just as she never failed to flutter her eyelids when he added, "And it's all thanks to you."

Then came the Silvener party. Every year, on roughly the same date, François Silvener entertained Limoges and the surrounding countryside. It was the most elegant occasion of the season and Odile, throwing all scruple to the winds, had been looking forward to it for the past ten days. It was also the one evening for which Gilles had decided to sacrifice his solitude. He wanted to see where Nathalie lived. He wanted to see her as a hostess, a prospect that amused him.

François Silvener's house was a large eighteenth-century structure, which must always have belonged to a member of the judiciary. Right in the center of Limoges, it opened on a large garden which, although very beautiful, was a little too lit up for the occasion. There were too many flowers, too, thought Gilles as he climbed the steps, and something that gave off the odor of money. Respectable money, to be sure, inherited money, but money nevertheless: the solid, gleaming furniture, the period carpets, the huge glittering mirrors, the two red-faced major-domos, awkward in their gloves, behind the buffet, everything bespoke a well-ordered provincial opulence. Gilles, as a journalist and a Parisian, had been to far more sumptuous, more ostentatious parties, often given by otherwise ruined playboys. He felt slightly superior. He only liked money when it was being squandered. It was not the luxury that was suffocating here, it was the impression of security. At the head of the staircase, as in a novel of the 1900's, Nathalie and François Silvener stood side by side receiving their guests. And there was a look in Nathalie's eyes when he came to kiss her hand which showed such anxiety to please him, an expression which so manifestly signified, "All this is for you," that he suddenly felt ashamed of his condescension. He congratulated her as warmly as possibly on the beauty of her house, shook Silvener's hand and went into the main reception room.

It was already teeming with rapturous guests and he had to submit to a certain amount of small talk and several compliments on how well he was looking before he could make his way toward what was evidently a library. He tried to imagine Nathalie in that chair by the corner of the fireplace, opposite her husband; but no, it was impossible. He could only visualize Nathalie lying on her back in the big, solitary bed in the hot bedroom, or stretched out on the grass. He took à few deep breaths and moved toward the balcony, bumping into someone on the way. It was the man he had privately nicknamed "the baby brother," since hearing Nathalie's tales. They had met only once, but Pierre Lacour immediately held out his hand. The baby brother was singularly tall and masculine-looking, thought Gilles, and very handsome into the bargain. He remembered how jealous of him he had been that day, and smiled.

"We despaired of seeing you," said Lacour. "You're not very social. I see your sister everywhere, but you, never."

"It's true, I'm not very social," said Gilles.

"Perhaps our provincial parties bore you?"

There was a hint of aggressiveness in his voice, but Gilles was anxious to make friends with him.

"Not in the least. I got run down in Paris and came here for a rest."

There was a brief silence, then Pierre Lacour seemed to come to a sudden decision. He took Gilles by the arm.

"I'd like to talk to you. You know that I'm . . . er . . . devoted to my sister?"

"Yes," said Gilles, smiling, "I know."

He was not going to act the innocent. Either the boy knew everything or he knew nothing. Besides, there was something about his face that Gilles found instantly attractive, a kind of awkward honesty combined with great intelligence. Nevertheless, his opening words were disconcerting.

"Nathalie loves you," he said abruptly. "And I deeply regret it."

He had turned away as he said this, and Gilles wondered for a moment if he had heard right.

"Why do you regret it?"

"Because I haven't much respect for you, if you'll forgive my saying so."

They were speaking in low voices in this dimly lit room, like two enemies plotting a secret and inevitable duel. Gilles's pulse quickened.

"Why don't you have any respect for me? I hardly know you."

"Nathalie loves you, and you say you love her. What is she doing here? Do you take her for one of those vulgar little women who make a habit of adultery? Do you imagine her situation with François is pleasant? Don't you know her better than that?"

"She decided to wait until the end of the summer. . . ." began Gilles.

Pierre Lacour made an impatient gesture.

"She hasn't decided anything at all. She thinks you don't know your own mind, and she doesn't want to put pressure on you. That's all. For the past month she's been living under false pretenses, something quite alien to her. All because of you."

Gilles was getting irritated. This "big brother" act was going a bit too far.

"I gather I wasn't her first adventure. . . ."

"No. But certainly her first real passion. And I'm worried to death for her."

"Why, may I ask?"

"Because you're weak, selfish, vacillating. . . ."

"All men are," said Gilles drily.

"But they're not all so complacent about it."

They were close to blows. Gilles tried to keep calm. The boy was both right and wrong. He took a deep breath.

"What would you do if you were in my place?"

"I would never be in your place: if I were another man and Nathalie weren't my sister, I would have taken her away long ago."

He had raised his voice and Gilles smiled:

"My God, you really love her. . . ."

"It's I who should be saying that to you, don't you think?"

There was silence.

"But I do love her," said Gilles gently.

"Then take care of her."

The furious look had gone, giving way to a sad, imploring, almost humble expression, an expression Gilles had seen before, on Nathalie's face. Something tugged at his heart.

"You think I should take her away? Tomorrow?"

"Yes," said Lacour. "As soon as possible. She is too unhappy."

They stared at one another for a moment. A few feet away could be heard the cheerful hubbub of the Silvener party. Suddenly Gilles was stirred by a romantic, lyrical impulse.

"All right, I will," he said. "And I'll take good care of her."

Already, in his mind's eye, he saw himself crossing the ballroom floor, seizing Nathalie by the wrist and dragging her off without a word, to the stupefaction of the guests. He had sailed straight into a nineteenth-century dream world. Lacour's voice brought him up sharply:

"Silvener is a good man. She must leave him properly. If it's possible to leave someone properly."

The memory of Eloise crossed Gilles's mind, and he did not reply.

"Don't forget, she's passionate and uncompromising," said Lacour in a low voice.

He crossed in front of Gilles and vanished. The past few minutes had been like a dream. The boy must be slightly mad. But Gilles's eyes had been opened. And, kissing Nathalie's hand at the end of the evening, leaving her to stand at the head of the staircase with her husband, in her own home, realizing that this woman who belonged to him could not follow him right then and there and was as despairing about it as he, he made his decision.

PART FIVE

Paris

20

"But what happened?"

They were in his flat in Paris. She had just arrived, after he had waited three days without news of her. Now here she was, looking dazed and placid at the same time, like someone who has been hit over the head. She had arrived without warning, had dropped her suitcase in the hall and her coat over a chair, and seemed ready to leave again. She did not even look round the flat, which was a little strange considering that she would be living there with him from now on, and that the decision was one they had taken together, the day after the party in Limoges, in a sort of rapture, a happiness both sober and profound. Gilles had not known that happiness could include that relentless and gentle wisdom which comes of doing unprotestingly what has to be done. But she had sent him ahead nevertheless—out of decorum, she said—and it was only now, three days later, that, half-crazed with worry, he found this mute creature on his doorstep, unannounced. He took her hand, sat her down, and poured her a drink, but she still said nothing.

"Do answer me. What happened?"

"Nothing," she said, almost irritably. "I spoke to François, I saw my brother, he drove me to the train, I didn't have time to let you know, I had the address, I took a taxi. . . ."

"Supposing I hadn't been here? . . ."

"You told me you'd be waiting for me."

Something in Nathalie's eyes, doubtless the recollection of painful scenes, indescribable, made him see his own enforced waiting, a bachelor's tense and lonely ordeal, as insignificant. After all, she had given up an entire life while he had been bored. You couldn't compare them: there was a slight difference between rereading old newspapers and telling your husband you no longer loved him. He bent down and kissed her on the cheek.

"How did he react?"

She looked at him in astonishment.

"What can it matter to you? You never cared what he was like when I was still living with him, did you? So why should how we parted matter to you? . . ."

"I just wondered if he . . . if it wasn't too painful, especially for you. . . ."

"Oh, me," she said, "I was leaving him for a man I love. He was being left on his own. You see . . ."

A vaguely cynical thought crossed Gilles's mind. Ultimately, an abandoned husband was more of a nuisance than one who was on the scene, emotionally speaking. Nathalie was trembling slightly, he could feel her cold hands in his, and he found himself half hoping that she would break down, burst into tears, tell him everything; or that she would throw herself into his arms and give herself to him in one of those surges of sensuality that are often touched off, after the event, by cruelty toward someone else. What he could not bear was this shivering, chaste, silent creature.

"You're frightened," he said. "You're not yourself. Come and see my little home." With uncharacteristic zest he had got the place ready for her, buying tea, Kleenex, biscuits, armfuls of flowers, and a new record. The concierge had done the cleaning and the concierge's husband had put in new electric light bulbs and got the refrigerator going again. Not for a moment had he imagined Nathalie's unhappiness. Or rather, he had imagined it in theatrical terms, full of ups and downs, changing moods, violent tears, streaked with drama of a "newsworthy" kind, palpitating with emotion. He had not imagined this silent misery.

She got up and followed him mechanically. In fact there was nothing to see apart from the kitchen, the bedroom, and the little bathroom that was finished in wood (an artistic innovation of Eloise's). She glanced at everything in a polite, absent-minded way. Nobody who saw her would have guessed she was going to sleep in this bed, hang up her clothes in this wardrobe; nobody, not even Gilles. He was seized with panic. What if she had been unable to go through with it? What if she had simply come in order to tell him (because it would have been inconceivable for her to telephone or to write), had simply taken the train in order to tell him she was not going to join him? And suddenly the flowers he had bought, the double bed turned down ready for her, the job in September, the coming winter, the whole of life seemed hateful, unbearable to Gilles. He took her by the arm and turned her towards him.

"Do you like it here?"

"Yes, of course," she said, "it's charming."

It was the word "charming" that convinced him. This silence of hers, this lack of any gesture toward him, these cold hands, this faraway look . . . Nathalie no longer loved him. Those three days of anxious, panic-stricken waiting he had endured, three days spent flinging newspapers on the floor, picking up and putting down the telephone, they had been a premonition. He would be alone once more, she was going to leave him. He turned away from her and went over to the window. Night had fallen, but summer lingered in the streets. He was alone.

"Gilles," she said.

He turned around. She had taken off her shoes, and was lying stretched out on the bed. No, she was not going to leave at once, she was going to spend an evening, a night with "her love, her dearest love" as she called him, and she would tell him in the morning, before she left. She was honest all right, but there are things one cannot do without. He felt the anger welling up inside him, and moving away from the window, he sat down on the edge of the bed. She looked beautiful lying there, tired, distracted, indifferent even. He loved her.

"You called me?"

She looked at him, surprised, and stretched out her hand toward him. He caught it in midair and gripped it tight.

"So you're offering me one last night? And tomorrow you'll explain that it's too hard on François, that you're too set in your ways, etc. . . . And you'll be off. Isn't that it?"

In his anger, he was hoping to see her face crumple under the impact of the truth and surprise at his intuition. But she simply went on staring at him, her eyes widening, until suddenly they filled with tears without her face moving a muscle, and he knew he had been wrong. He slumped down beside her, overwhelmed with shame and relief, and buried his head in her shoulder. He was unable to speak. It was she who murmured:

"My God, Gilles, how self-centered you are. . . ."

"I was so frightened," he said. "Three whole days. And then, just now . . . You won't ever leave me?"

There was a short silence. Then Nathalie's familiar voice, restored to her at last, a voice half tender, half teasing:

"No, not unless you want me to."

"I couldn't bear it," he said. "I've only just begun to realize that."

He lay there without moving, inhaling her familiar scent, the scent that would always be associated in his mind with the countryside, fresh grass, and the empty bedroom underneath the roof. It seemed strange, almost sacrilegious, to be breathing it here, in this city bedroom through which so many women had passed and in which Eloise had lived. Seen thus, half hidden by Nathalie's shoulder and in the aura of her perfume, it no longer looked the same. He too was a stranger here, as well as this scared woman. They could as well have been in some hotel, like unhappy lovers in a Piaf song. Yet they were reunited and at home. What was the cause of his disquiet? He felt a tightening of the throat that seemed to spring from something other than the panic of recent days, from something other than anger or grief, from something far more profound, unknown, like an immense foreboding.

He clung to her with a low moan, murmuring words of tenderness. Nathalie's hand was resting on the back of his neck, she was breathing gently, and he realized that she was asleep. He got up and went to the refrigerator, opened the bottle of champagne he had put there, poured a large glassful, and returned to the foot of the bed. Nathalie's face was trusting, weary, gentle. Suddenly he raised his glass above her, swore that he would never do her any harm, and took an immense gulp of cold champagne. At once he was reminded of the glass of warm beer he had swallowed in one gulp when he had confessed his love for this woman in the café with Jean. A month ago, but it might have been ten years. Now she was here, in his home, she was his, he had won. And he could not refrain from smiling: at his own blindness, his own stubbornness, his own sense of responsibility, his follies, his victories.

21

"I haven't given you the news about Eloise," Jean said with a laugh. "I suppose he's told you about poor Eloise?"

Nathalie nodded and smiled. The three of them were in a little restaurant on the river, and Jean and Nathalie seemed to be getting on splendidly. Gilles was delighted.

"I was certain he would have. Gilles never knows when to keep quiet. The only time he really tried was in your case. That's how I knew he was in love with you, and forced him to admit it. But I don't suppose he told you about that?"

"That's enough," said Gilles.

But he smiled benignly. After all, it was a highly enjoyable pastime, albeit an adolescent one, listening to your mistress and your best friend making affectionate fun of you. You felt somehow outside it all, like some strange, fragile, elusive object, but eventually you identified yourself with this object they were describing, and you felt important and loved.

"Well, I'm going to disappoint you. Eloise's career is progressing like lightning. She's the mistress of the top photographer at *Vogue* and everything's going splendidly Look at him, Nathalie, he's furious. He'd like women to weep for him the rest of their lives."

"I couldn't care less," said Gilles.

"Neither would I, if I were in your place," said Jean, taking Nathalie's hand and kissing it. She smiled at him. For the past week they had wandered round Paris, deserted for the month of August; for the past week they had slept together every night in the double bed in the rue Monsieur le Prince, and she had seemed perfectly happy. They had seen no one, apart from Jean, who had returned the previous day. Only, when Jean had called for them a couple of hours earlier, she had behaved as though she were a chance guest at the flat, and it was Gilles who had to serve the drinks, fetch the ice, etc. He must remember to ask her why.

"I must drop in at the Club later on," said Jean. "Has Nathalie been there yet? No? You must come and see what's in store for you in the evenings, with this layabout."

Nathalie left to comb her hair. Jean watched her go, a hint of melancholy overshadowing his plump features.

"She's pretty stunning looking," he said.

"Do you think so?" said Gilles in a little, fluting, faraway voice which made them both laugh.

"She's better than you," Jean went on meditatively, "much better. And I don't mean physically," he added.

"Thanks," said Gilles.

"Try not to . . ." Jean began. Then he stopped and shook his head.

"I know," said Gilles cheerfully, "try not to make her unhappy, try to keep her as she is, try not to be selfish, try to behave like a real man, etc."

"Yes," said Jean, "try."

They looked each other in the eye, then simultaneously turned away. There were moments when Gilles could not bear his reflection in Jean's eyes. As soon as Nathalie returned, they got up and left.

The Club was gay and already crowded. It seemed that August no longer existed for some Parisians. They were greeted by a sun-tanned Pierre, who pressed Gilles to his bosom, calling him "my boy," seemed wholly oblivious of having punched him in the mouth the last time they met, and threw an appreciative, inquiring glance in Nathalie's direction. Gilles hesitated. With any other woman he would have said, "Nathalie, this is Pierre," and that would have been that: Gilles Lantier's new mistress was called Nathalie. But he couldn't. He said in a pompous voice: "May I introduce Pierre Leroux? Madame Silvener." Then he blushed.

He went through the same ceremony a dozen times in the course of the evening. Everyone came and slapped him on the shoulder, the girls kissed him in accordance with the rules of mutual affection current at the time, and each time he disengaged himself from a powerful or delicate arm— depending on the sex (though even so not necessarily)—he would turn to Nathalie and introduce him or her to Madame Silvener. Each time, it was obvious that this simple formality caused raised eyebrows, but he persisted nonetheless, much to Jean's amusement and Nathalie's utter incomprehension. Naturally good old Nicholas, the drunken old pal, turned up, too, and having been duly introduced, observed to Nathalie:

"So you're the one who kidnapped him? We were worried, you know. Mind you, if I'd been him I'd never have come back."

He gave an amiable leer and calmly sat down at their table.

"How about standing me a drink to celebrate?"

"We weren't celebrating anything," said Gilles irritably, "except some peace and quiet until you arrived."

"My, my!" said Nicholas, thick-skinned and anyway thirsty, "I do believe he's jealous. I'm sure Madame will be delighted if we drink to her first visit to the Club. . . . I haven't seen you here before, have I? I'd certainly remember if I had, believe you me. . . ."

Still smiling amorously at Nathalie, he appropriated the bottle on the table and poured himself a large whiskey. Gilles was furious, and became even more so when he saw Jean on the other side of the table screwing up his eyes, trying not to laugh. Nathalie, next to him, said nothing.

"Look here, Nicholas," he said, "we're talking shop."

"If you're talking shop, Madame must be bored. Will you dance with me, Madame?"

Nathalie suddenly burst out laughing, and Jean with her. They could not stop. With unaffected good humor, Nicholas joined in, taking the opportunity of helping himself to another drink. Gilles was left alone with his respectability, humiliated and enraged.

"If you could only see your face . . ." Jean chortled.

Nathalie's eyes were brimming with tears of laughter and Gilles managed to force a stiff little smile. He was sorely tempted to leave these two idiots and go and get drunk with his old friends at another table. It was after all a long time since he had been in Paris. And if all his efforts to spare his mistress's feelings led to this, he might as well stop trying. It was simple.

"Why don't you go and dance?" he asked Nathalie.

"I can't dance that," she said, "as you well know. You must forgive me," she said to Nicholas, "I'm a country bumpkin."

"Really," said Nicholas, "where are you from?"

"The Limousin."

"The Limousin? I adore the Limousin. I've even got relations there. Fancy that . . . That calls for a drink. Gilles, let's drink to the Limousin."

Whereupon, to the consternation of Gilles, Nathalie and Nicholas embarked on a long conversation about the charms of the countryside, haymaking, the corn harvest, and the wine harvest, which last, so it seemed, had especially appealed to Nicholas. It was two in the morning when Jean, himself cheerfully tipsy, dropped them off at home. Nathalie was a little unsteady and Gilles was like a bear with a sore head. He thought up a few cutting phrases in the bathroom, but when he came back to the bedroom she was already fast asleep. He lay down beside her, and it was a long time before he could get to sleep.

22

She awoke next morning with the wide-eyed, sheepish look of someone who, in spite of a glass or two too many and a slight feeling of guilt, has slept like a log and feels full of beans. She gave him a sly look and he couldn't help smiling.

"Well," he said, "did you have sweet dreams about Nicholas?"

"I adore Nicholas," she said. "He's like a great big dog."

"Yes, a great big drunken dog," said Gilles. "By the way, I didn't know you drank."

She looked at him and hesitated.

"It's because," she said, "it's because I was so shy. I didn't know a soul and you knew everyone. And I looked so ridiculous among all those girls. . . ."

Gilles stared at her, appalled.

"Yes, I was wearing my little black dress and my pearls, and they were all got up like Diana the Huntress or something. And you looked so embarrassed introducing me to everyone. . . ."

"That's the limit," said Gilles. "That's really the limit. Do you honestly think I could be ashamed of you?"

He turned over in bed and took her in his arms. She had been scared. . . . Nathalie, who was never scared of anything, who had defied the whole of Limousin society, who had left her husband, Nathalie had been frightened of a roomful of amiable drunks. He wanted to laugh and cry at the same time.

"Not ashamed exactly," she said dreamily. "Not ashamed, but you might have been bored. That's why I was so pleased when Nicholas came and sat down with us."

"What about Jean? He thinks you're marvelous."

"But, Jean is your friend, first and foremost. Whatever you do to him or to me, he'll forgive you for. I even wonder whether, in an odd way, he doesn't enjoy seeing you behave badly."

"You're mad," Gilles said.

Nevertheless he now remembered the occasional look of glee on Jean's face when he, Gilles, was in the middle of what they used to call his "moments of crisis," and every kind of outrageous and foolish behavior seemed acceptable to him. Jean would calm him down, reason with him, but with a sort of amused, almost admiring tolerance which often spurred Gilles on to even worse excesses. One never knows anything about one's friends, nor about the subterranean influence—unknown even to them occasionally—they have over you. Nevertheless, the idea of Jean, good old Jean, as an evil genius was pretty comic. He began to laugh.

"You analyze everything. Do you mean to turn my whole life upside down?"

"I wouldn't have said you'd exactly spared mine," she said calmly.

She looked at him, smiling with half-closed eyes. She may have been afraid of all those people the night before, but she was manifestly not in the least afraid of him this morning.

"You're a hard woman," he said. "You're not afraid of anything. And what's more, you're an alcoholic. And what's even more, you're perverse," he concluded, flinging himself on top of her. "You ought to meet Gilda."

"Who's Gilda?"

He felt her body against his: he wanted her, and did not in the least want to talk about Gilda. Nevertheless he replied vaguely:

"A perverted woman."

"Oh," she said, "all women can be perverted. Me too, you know. Perversions don't mean a thing. . . . Anything goes, when you love someone. . . ."

"Shut up," he said, "chatterbox."

They lunched, very late, at the Brasserie Lipp and Gilles made more introductions, this time with perfect naturalness. He would be starting work in three days' time, his mistress was beautiful, and she loved him; he was happy. He wondered how the wretched, shivering specter of three months ago could possibly have been he. He must have been physically done in at the time without realizing it. Today the world was at his feet. He wanted champagne; it was ludicrous drinking champagne with sauerkraut, but champagne they duly drank.

Then they went to see an idiotic film in the neighborhood and Gilles whiled away the time whispering inane comments in Nathalie's furious ear, for she was as attentive and serious as a child at any sort of show. For the past three days, she had been nagging Gilles to take her to an intellectual play that was said to be very good, the mere idea of which made Gilles's blood run cold. It was years since he had been to the theater—he loathed evenings planned in advance—and he teased her for what he called her provincialism.

"You've got plenty of time," he said. "You're not in Paris for a week. You don't have to see everything in a few days so that you can tell the Red Cross ladies of Limoges all about it."

"But I enjoy it," she said. "You don't understand. And it's with you that I'd like to talk about it afterward."

"That's cheerful," he groaned, "I've landed myself with an intellectual."

"I've never tried to hide it from you," she retorted solemnly, and the idea of Nathalie, his mistress, that warm, demanding body, transformed into an intellectual made him laugh until he cried. At times, however, when some chance remark made him aware of the range and depth of her culture by comparison with his, he was a little surprised. True, she had had the time to read during thirty years in the provinces, but she did in fact genuinely enjoy it; and when in a tired moment he let slip some fashionable paradox or commonplace, she would take him up on it mercilessly, with a sort of irritated astonishment, as though he had suddenly proved unworthy of himself.

"My darling," he would say (although convinced of the opposite), "I'm not an intelligent man. You'll just have to face it."

"You could be," she would retort coldly, "if you hadn't given up using your intelligence on anything but your private life. You have no curiosity. I sometimes wonder why they keep you on that newspaper."

135

"Because I work hard, behave nicely, and type beautifully."

She shrugged and laughed, but there was a touch of rancor in her laughter. Gilles was always delighted when they reached this point. He had always enjoyed being "scolded." Naturally it all ended up with loving words and caresses, and once he had her at his mercy, swooning with desire, Gilles would ask her in a staccato voice if she liked what her stupid lover did to her. They were at that exquisite stage when lovers adore to argue and cannot begin to imagine that the subjects of their tender quarrels may be the germ, the harbingers, of less carefree battles to come.

23

For the first time since he had started work two months before he wanted to have a drink alone in a bar before going home. It was very pleasant to act the part of the care-free young bachelor when someone you loved, someone you were sure of, was waiting for you somewhere. The cafés of Paris were bottomless pits for lonely men, but springboards for happy lovers. He even took time to flirt with the barmaid and leaf through the evening paper. He didn't ask himself why he was not going straight home; he was simply grateful to Nathalie because, thanks to her, this absurd loitering he was allowing himself before going back to her was a rich and happy symbol of his freedom. One is never free except in relation to someone else. And when, as in his case, the relation is based on happiness, it allows the greatest freedom in the world. He had worked hard all day, and that evening he was to dine with Fairmont, Jean, and Nathalie. They didn't yet know whether Fairmont would bring his wife. Probably not, since he and Jean would be bringing their respective mistresses. He ought to hurry back and change. But in this bar he had a feeling of casualness, of insouciance, which he found hard to shake off. When he got back, Nathalie would doubtless be there, mildly exhausted by her endless exploration of Paris, embarked on day after day with an enthusiasm which never flagged and which left him a little more skeptical each time. She now knew streets, cafés, art galleries that he had never even heard of and he wondered, with a mixture of anxiety and impatience, when she would have done with this city, and what she would do then. They dined out every night, and occasionally called in at the Club, where, taking refuge in total indifference toward the amusing people to whom he introduced her and a Tolstoyan affection for Nicholas, she devoted herself exclusively to the latter and to him. He noticed incidentally and with some astonishment that that great booby Nicholas was extremely well-read, was not undiscriminating, was comparatively sober, and was visibly falling in love with Nathalie. In the long run he found it all quite enjoyable: instead of gossiping about the private habits of some fashionable actor, they would talk about those of a Zola hero, and although there was little likelihood of anything very new emerging, he nevertheless learned a good deal. Afterward Nathalie would proclaim vehemently that it was really shameful that Nicholas couldn't find a producer with enough intelligence to trust him with a few hundred thousand francs and that it was remarkable he wasn't more embittered, and he let her run on, if anything rather amused, reluctant to point out to her that Nicholas was notoriously as idle as a slug, that he was a confirmed alcoholic with six unsuccessful cures be-

hind him, and that for the past ten years he had been impotent in every sense of the word. Sometimes Jean would
join them with his bovine Marthe, who was visibly appalled
by Nathalie, as though by some impropriety: women, in her
view, ought to be seen and not heard. And occasionally
Jean's expression betrayed a somewhat similar disapproval.
But Gilles knew why: for fifteen years they had talked to
one another over the heads of submissive and desirable
young women; suddenly to find sitting between them one
who was both desirable and alive was bound to arouse his
jealousy. The sort of jealousy between friends which is often
the worst. But Gilles, affable and rather proud, listened to
Nathalie's questions, rejoinders, and sometimes sharp rebut-
tals without turning a hair. In an hour or two she would be
his, submissive as she would never be in other circumstances, and that amply sufficed him. He knew that this
Minerva would quickly transform herself into a lover. And
if she had not yet adopted the pants suits or the high boots of
the Club girls, her proud head, her green eyes, the sort of
contained violence in her body, soon made one forget the
little black dress and the antiquated necklace to which she
still clung. In fact, Gilles found a certain erotic excitement
in watching and listening to this slightly old-fashioned
woman talking passionately about Balzac and addressing all
these cheerful, gossipy, familiar night owls with the formal
"vous," knowing that, in a few hours' time, this same woman
would be naked and doubtless more uninhibited in her love-
making than any of these up-to-date girls. In any case, the
eloquent stares of the few genuine connoisseurs of women
who frequented the Club had made it clear to him that he
was envied.

The dinner took place in a smart restaurant on the Right

Bank and, because of Gilles, they arrived a little late. Fairmont had come alone and he apologized for his wife's absence in a phrase which made Gilles and Jean exchange a smile. He glanced at Nathalie with some surprise, having no doubt expected a starlet, and ordered dinner with a slightly perplexed air. Marthe, probably briefed by Jean, gazed at him with a look of such steadfast admiration that Gilles wanted to laugh. He knew that Fairmont was pleased with him and that Nathalie was curious to meet Fairmont, so all would be well. And indeed, to begin with, everything did go well. Fairmont asked Nathalie if she liked the restaurant, to which she replied that she had been there a few times with her husband and that the oysters were delicious. Fairmont, apparently in the picture, asked the inevitable questions about the Limousin and Nathalie replied briefly, after which the conversation developed along the most general and innocuous lines. As it happened, Nathalie and Fairmont did most of the talking, and he was soon looking at her with a slightly quizzical air, as though wondering what she could possibly see in a man like Gilles. Nathalie, sensing this, gave her lover a smile so tender that he took her hand under the table for a moment. Now Fairmont was out to please and began to hold forth, having drunk a fair amount. Marthe's goggling eyes were closing under the strain.

"The situation is very tricky for us," Fairmont was saying. "Events are so contradictory . . ."

"They always are," said Nathalie.

"However," said Fairmont crisply, "as Stendhal said, 'the heart must either break or turn to stone.'"

"It was Chamfort, I think," said Nathalie.

"Excuse me?"

Fairmont sat stock-still, his fork in midair. He was perfectly willing to invite his colleagues to dinner, and even their mistresses, but he did not appreciate lessons in culture. Gilles gave Nathalie a kick and she looked at him, surprised.

"I'm sorry to contradict you," said Fairmont firmly, "but it was Stendhal. In fact, I believe it's in *La Chartreuse*," he added in a ruminative voice which terrified Gilles, since it indicated a slight doubt—which proved that Nathalie was right.

"In any case it's a marvelous remark," he said hurriedly.

"If you'll allow me, I shall look it up," said Fairmont, addressing himself to Nathalie. And turning to Gilles he added, in the suave tone he adopted when he was angry, "Anyway, I'm delighted to see that you know a cultivated young woman. It's a change."

There was a short silence. Gilles bowed.

"Thank you," he said.

Now *he* was rather angry. With Fairmont whom he considered rude and with Nathalie whom he considered tactless. Nathalie too had flushed slightly; there was an awkward silence and at the precise moment when Gilles was about to go into raptures over the consistency of the soufflé, he heard Nathalie's voice beside him:

"I'm sorry," she said. "If I had thought that correcting a quotation would irritate you so much, I would have kept quiet."

"Nothing that a beautiful woman says could irritate me," said Fairmont, with a little smile.

"I'll end up as a messenger on this paper," thought Gilles with an imploring glance at Jean, who was following it all with an impassive air. Impassive and also secretly delighted—but was it at seeing Fairmont snubbed or at seeing Nathalie put him, Gilles, in an embarrassing position?

The rest of the meal was somewhat flat and they took leave of one another very early. When they were alone together in the flat, Nathalie turned to him.

"You're angry, aren't you? He was infuriating, too. . . . I've seldom met such a pretentious man."

"All the same, he's our bread and butter," said Gilles.

"That's no reason for mixing up Stendhal and Chamfort," she said tranquilly, "especially not in that stupid, dogmatic way. . . ."

"Stupid or not, he's my boss," said Gilles.

He was annoyed at hearing himself say such things. He felt like a "young executive" or an "old retainer." At any rate, not like the brilliant, devil-may-care reporter he wanted to be. And all because of this woman standing there, smiling. Why couldn't she play the game? She knew perfectly well that the world is what it is and that there are times when one has to compromise, to suppress one's real feelings, and perhaps laugh at one's own cowardice later on. One could not play the incorruptible in Paris in the year of grace 1967, not in his job. It was obvious, and there was a sort of dishonesty in not admitting it. Why did she have to apply to everything those absolute values of hers, her horror of the half measures which, whether we like it or not, alone permit us to lead a quiet life? He felt as though she had let him down, and told her so.

"If I liked half measures," she answered, "I wouldn't be here. I'd be in Limoges and I'd come up and make love to you once a fortnight."

"You're confusing feelings with grand gestures," he said. "You came here because you loved me and I loved you, and there was nothing else to do. There was no such necessity, this evening, in your behavior toward Fairmont."

142

"I simply meant that if I could have stood that man, I could just as easily have stood my past life, that's all."

Something stirred in Gilles, a sort of exasperated rancor such as he had never detected in himself before.

"In short, you're pleased with your role: the woman who leaves everything for her lover, who spends her time in museums swooning in front of works of art, who discovers Chekhovian heroes in the Nicholases of this world, the sublime, intransigent woman, involved by chance with a wretched scribbler who is weak and of inferior caliber, the true woman, passionate, understanding, the woman who ..."

"Yes," she interrupted, "I know I'm a rather headstrong woman. But for one thing, I'm not proud of it, and for another I thought it was one of the things you loved me for."

"As a matter of fact, it's true," he said thoughtfully. "You're always right."

"Gilles," she said.

He looked at her. There was a look of desperate panic in her eyes. He took her in his arms. He really was behaving like a swine. He left her on her own day after day in a strange town, he took her to dine with commonplace people, and then he complained about her behavior. Perhaps she was bored to death in Paris, perhaps her desperate efforts to maintain some semblance of dignity in her role as official mistress of a man like himself were due to an instinct of self-preservation as vital to her as her passion for him. . . . Why wouldn't she marry him? He had suggested it to her a dozen times and each time she had refused: for his sake, moreover, he was sure. And it was true, he was afraid of marrying, for stupid, bourgeois reasons, under the pretext of avoiding just that bourgeois state. She ought to have said "yes," got a divorce, and dragged him to the registry office by the scruff of his neck, whatever fears or reservations she sensed in him. There are times when one must force people, when one must deliberately refuse to understand them, when one must take the initiative, against their wishes, but in the long run for their own good. But that she could never do, and that was why he loved her. The two were inextricable.

"Come to bed," he said tenderly. "It's late."

In bed, at least, there would be no more problems. And she obviously shared his thought, for she was even more passionate, more loving, than ever. Nevertheless, at about five o'clock in the morning, he awoke to find Nathalie sitting up in bed beside him, motionless, her eyes wide open, smoking a cigarette in the dark. He wanted to wake up properly and talk to her, but something made him close his eyes again and keep silent, like a coward. They would talk it over in the morning—if there was anything to talk over.

24

"Won't you have a little cognac? We've got the time."

"I'd gladly have a dozen cognacs," thought Gilles angrily. They were in one of those restaurants where one must try the *terrine* at all costs, and in a quarter of an hour they would be sitting in the theater watching the famous play Nathalie had been wanting to see. She had run into a childhood friend in Paris, a plain, intelligent woman disastrously married to a loud-mouthed and bibulous businessman. It was Nathalie who had arranged the evening, warning him beforehand about the boring husband, and once seated at the table she had chirped away gaily with her old friend about episodes in their childhood, leaving Gilles and the oaf to their own devices. Having reviewed the stock exchange, taxes, restaurants, and Gaullism, Gilles felt on the verge of hysteria.

"Just take it from your old pal Roger—you don't mind if

I call you Gilles—I can tell you we're going to need it. The theater sends me to sleep instantly. And my wife drags me there once a month at the very least."

"That's something we've got in common," thought Gilles sourly, "poor workingmen whose womenfolk drag them out at night."

"Especially when there's television," Roger went on. "It may not be all that hot, I know, but sometimes you see some damned interesting things. You're sitting in a comfortable armchair, you can smoke, you can drink, you're in your own home, and you don't have to pay thirty smackers for the privilege of being bored stiff. Don't you agree?"

"I like the theater," said Gilles firmly. "But I'll have a cognac all the same."

"And do you remember . . ." began Nathalie. "What are you two talking about?"

She gave Gilles a pleading look, a look of apology.

"We were talking about the theater," he said sarcastically. "Monsieur—sorry, Roger—prefers television."

"I have a terrible job getting him to go out," said the childhood friend. "We have a compact—once a month, I drag him to the theater by force."

"That's how we'll end up," Gilles said to Nathalie with a disagreeable smile. "Such compacts are the lifeblood of a marriage."

She did not smile. There was a look of such obvious distress on her face, so animated a moment before, that Gilles was stricken with remorse. After all, this wretched girl friend was the only person she knew in Paris; it wasn't her fault that the husband was what he was; and she was delighted to be going to the theater. Why should he spoil her evening?

"Would you like a cognac?" he asked.

He reached for her hand across the table, and smiled at her. She looked at him gratefully and Gilles felt a sudden pang. He was making her unhappy, or he was going to make her unhappy, he knew it. What harm would one boring evening do to him, after all? She must have put up with many in the past three months with *his* friends. Still, it must be admitted that none of them had this man Roger's appalling garrulousness; you really had to be from the provinces to know Parisians like him.

"We must hurry," said Nathalie's friend. "You can't imagine," she said to Gilles, "how delighted I am that Nathalie is living in Paris at last. We'll see each other often, I hope? . . ."

Her voice had a slightly anxious, questioning note. She must know the sort of man she had married. One couldn't blame her. It was only natural: a plain girl in the provinces, a Parisian passing through. But however natural it was, Gilles resented the implied parallel between her situation and Nathalie's. True, they were dressed more or less alike and their animated discussion about their school days would have been unthinkable between two Parisians, usually far too preoccupied with their menfolk for such irrelevancies. But Nathalie was beautiful, she was not bourgeois, she loved him. He smiled.

"Of course. But we'll go and see a Western occasionally, for a change."

"There was one on TV tonight," Roger complained. "Next time, old man, we'll make a bachelor evening of it at home and send the women off to see their theatricals. What do you think?"

Gilles was so visibly appalled at the thought of such an evening that Nathalie broke into a nervous giggle. She was still chuckling to herself in the theater, and she took his hand in the dark. He slid it under her coat and onto her thigh, to disturb and annoy her, but she was no longer paying any attention to him, she was engrossed in the play, which was indeed very fine; but Gilles, his nerves on edge and his mind benumbed by that ghastly dinner, listened to it with only half an ear.

In the interval, they went to the bar for the obligatory whiskey, and while the two women argued passionately and Roger gloomily swallowed a few extra drinks, Gilles looked around him. It was as though all of provincial France had arranged to meet there. There were young couples and middle-aged couples, in twos or fours, all in their Sunday best, the women got up in skunk or mink, indifferently cut, delighted with themselves for being there and holding forth about the author's intentions with all the complacency and pretentiousness of the French middle class. He knew that, elegance apart, first-night audiences were no different, but elegance, genuine or acquired, suddenly seemed to him of utmost importance. One had to be either a snob or a communist, he thought, but he could not decide which. After the inevitable farewell drink in a gruesome bar near the theater, they finally separated. In the old Simca, which he had recovered at last, Gilles maintained a discreet and slightly sadistic silence. It was Nathalie who eventually broke it.

"You were dreadfully bored, weren't you?" she said mournfully.

"Not at all," said Gilles, "the play was very good. Shall we go to the Club and have a nightcap?"

"She was a very nice girl, you know," Nathalie went on without answering. "Very sweet and very romantic."

"She seems charming," said Gilles. "It's a pity she married that man."

"Yes. A great pity."

148

He turned toward her with a smile.

"Nathalie," he said, "do you realize that I love you?"

He did not know why he said this, he simply felt that he had to tell her. She took his hand off the steering wheel and squeezed it without replying. They arrived at the Club.

The smoke, the roar of excited voices, the familiar face of the girl at the door had the effect on Gilles of a breath of fresh air. Which was strange, when you came to think of it. They found a small table at once, and had two quick drinks in succession. Gilles was filled with a sense of gaiety and release: he felt like getting drunk, talking nonsense, picking a fight with someone for fun, doing whatever came into his head. Suddenly he saw Jean beckoning to them from the other end of the room, where he was sitting with a group of strangers. Gilles got up at once, dragging Nathalie behind him. He was back again among his natural friends, the nightbirds, the degenerates, the drunks, the layabouts. It was not until they had almost reached the table that he recognized Eloise. She looked ravishing and exotic in a very short leather skirt draped with chains. She smiled at him without constraint, gave Nathalie an approving glance, and introduced a tall, rather drunken American with the air some women assume when introducing their current lovers. Jean rose, smiling, and placed Nathalie next to him. She would be bound to talk to him about the play, and Jean enjoyed that sort of conversation, so all was well. He could amuse himself as he liked. The American had taken him by the shoulders and was trying, over the noise of the music, to tell him something he could not understand.

"Eloise and you? . . . Before? Yes?"

He pointed a finger at Eloise and Gilles in turn, smiling broadly. Gilles understood, and laughed too.

"Yes, it was me."

He caught Nathalie's eye and smiled. He was really rather pleased that she should meet Eloise, especially an Eloise looking as she did now. It was somehow flattering to him. And to her.

"He's the man who made me unhappy," Eloise shouted above the din.

"Bad guy," said the American, shaking Gilles by the shoulders. "And now, you all alone?"

"No," Gilles yelled, for the music was growing more deafening, "I love that lady."

"Which one?"

He pointed his finger at Nathalie, noticed her slightly horrified expression, and did not pursue the matter. She had understood what they were saying, but what of it? He was only telling an amiable fellow that he loved her. It wasn't an indiscretion, it was the sort of nocturnal warmth and familiarity that didn't mean a thing. He gulped down a large Scotch. God knows, after an evening like that he had a right to relax. In fact he richly deserved it.

"Did you enjoy the play?" asked Jean.

"Loved it," he said, "*mar*velous."

Jean grinned and turned back to Nathalie. Gilles felt immensely gay, irresponsible, above reproach. This evening which had begun so boringly was ending up well.

"You might dance with me," said Eloise, "for old times' sake."

He was a bad dancer and did not enjoy it, but what did that matter? He found himself swooping and gliding across the floor, surrounded by rather stationary couples. The men were staring at Eloise in her Tarzan's-wife getup.

"My God," she said, "your dancing certainly hasn't improved."

He laughed. He recognized the scent she was wearing. It was pleasant having all these women dotted through his life like landmarks.

"And what about the rest?" she asked.

"You've become very impertinent," he said. "But I can't go into details here."

After all, why not? It would be amusing to make love one day to this *nouvelle Héloïse*. That was rather a good pun; he explained it to her, but she didn't seem to understand. Nathalie would understand, Nathalie was cultivated. She was just passing him, in the arms of the American, who was staggering slightly. She looked rather bored. "Enjoy youself, can't you," he thought, with a sort of rage. "Go on, enjoy yourself." They were the first to get back to the table; Nathalie and the American were still dancing.

"Your girl doesn't seem to be enjoying herself," said Eloise.

"Your friend's probably treading on her toes," said Gilles.

"He's rather sweet," said Eloise.

Three months ago, she would never have called a man "sweet." "She must have got her ideas about men from me," thought Gilles. With a sudden rush of alcoholic sentimentality, he said:

"Tell me you're happy, Eloise."

"Certainly, if it'll give you any pleasure," she said drily, turning her head away. Just then, Nathalie's drooping, almost sorrowful profile crossed his field of vision and he gulped down another Scotch. Women were all the same, never happy. And it was always your fault. When it came down to it, there was nothing like one's pals, and he winked conspiratorially at Jean, who winked back. Nathalie returned and he stood up. She looked at him hesitantly.

"Aren't you tired?"

Now, just as he was finally beginning to enjoy himself, she wanted to go home.

"No," he said. "Come and dance."

It happened to be a slow fox trot, which had been popular that summer. Suddenly he remembered the outdoor party at the house near Limoges, and the dance he had demanded from Nathalie when he was so jealous of her brother. And those mad, furtive kisses they had exchanged behind a tree . . . Nathalie. She was swaying gently against him, and he wanted her, he loved her, his little provincial, his blue-stocking, his bacchante. He bent his head and whispered it in her ear; she put her head on his shoulder. Friends, ex-mistresses, partners in crime, all were forgotten; there was no one but her.

Much later, in the small hours, they emerged, and Nathalie had to drive the car. Although he could hardly stand, he was brimming over with words, and forceful if confused ideas. He knew exactly what was happening between them. As long as he had been ill and she had looked after him as though he were a child, he felt whole, integrated, fulfilled in their love. Now that it was his turn to look after her and protect her, he felt dissociated, split in two: on one side himself, the old Gilles, on the other, the lover of Nathalie. He explained all this in a thick voice while she was putting him to bed, but she made no reply. He was awakened at the crack of dawn by a florist's delivery boy bearing a huge sheaf of flowers, and Nathalie, yawning, told him the American had never stopped proposing to her all night.

25

All that day he chewed over his resentment. He always wound up looking like a fool with this woman. Not only did he know nothing about the theater, nothing about art and good taste, and not much about literature, but when he played around a bit on what he thought was his own territory, she mimicked on the sly. She must have had a good laugh watching him flirt with poor Eloise, whose rich lover, clearly no fool, was ready to leave her then and there for Nathalie. For beneath that impeccably aloof exterior was a kind of animal sensuality which the American, drunk though he was, had sensed unerringly. When Gilles came into their room that morning, looking like an idiot with the bouquet in his arms, she had burst out laughing before telling him what had happened. And he had sat on the end of the bed, muttering to himself, "Well I'll be damned!" until, still laughing, she had taken the flowers from him and gotten up to give him a kiss.

"But what did you say to him?"

"That he was very kind but my affections were engaged elsewhere. I didn't think of pointing at you," she added innocently.

"He's got a nerve," said Gilles, making an effort to laugh. Nevertheless, he was annoyed. No doubt about it, he would never look very good next to her. She loved him, of course, but fundamentally she was the stronger of the two. The thought that this was probably what had saved him three months ago momentarily crossed his mind, but at the same time he was looking for some way of proving the contrary. Thinking about it now, it was she who had taken the initiative from the very beginning of their relationship. The only thing he had done was speed up their departure. It was she who had chosen him, seduced him, persuaded him to live with her. And she would soon be dictating their entire way of life, if he gave her the chance. Witness the previous night. True, it was the first time in two months that she had imposed such a chore on him, but there had to be a first time for everything. From being a man with a grievance he was transforming himself into a man in chains. He found it impossible to work, was extremely bad-tempered, and decided to go to see Gilda. He hadn't even called to say hello to her since his return, which was not very nice of him; moreover, Gilda possessed two enormously valuable qualities: first, she was always on the man's side, and second, she knew how to keep her mouth shut. By six o'clock he was in her flat, remembering on the doorstep the dreadful evening he had spent there last spring, waiting for a woman to whom, in the end, he had not even opened the door. That, he realized, had been "before Nathalie" and for a moment he was tempted to say nothing. Nathalie was his secret, she belonged to him, he had no right to talk about her to anyone; it was a despicable thing to do and probably one of the few things she would never forgive him for. But he was already sitting in the big red armchair with an iced drink in his hands and, opposite him, this friendly, inquisitive woman, his old partner in amorous misconduct. He felt rejuvenated. A love affair was only a love affair, after all.

"Well?" said Gilda. "You look well, darling. I gather you're very happy."

"Very," he answered flatly.

She always knew everything.

"So what are you doing here?" She laughed. "When men come to see me, it's either to make love or to complain. You don't look especially passionate. So?"

"It's complicated," he began. . . .

Then he talked. He went on talking, altering the facts slightly in his own favor, and hating himself for doing so. By the time he had finished, he was thoroughly depressed.

She had listened without a word, her eyes half closed, smoking cigarette after cigarette, with what he thought of as her fortune-teller look. When he had finished, she got up, walked about the room waggling her hips slightly, returned to her chair and looked him in the eyes. Really she was rather absurd, and he wondered what he was doing there. She caught the glint of malice in his eye and said crossly:

"As I understand it, some woman has got you into her clutches and you don't know how to escape, is that it?"

A wave of fury swept over him.

"That's not it at all," he said, "I've left out the main thing. I haven't told you the main thing."

The main thing was Nathalie's warmth, the hollow of her neck where he laid his head to sleep, her unfailing tenderness, her utter loyalty, the overwhelming confidence he felt in her. Everything that this semiwhore of a kept woman with her cheap perversions could not begin to understand. But in that case what was he doing here?

"What's the main thing? She's gotten under your skin, is that it?"

He was on his feet, stammering, but whether with rage or shame he did not know.

"I haven't explained properly," he mumbled. "Forget it. I'm sorry."

"When she's gone back to her judge, come and see me again," she said. "You know I'm always here."

"Yes," he thought with hatred, "you're always here. You'll always be here to minister to the cowardice, squalor, and lechery of your men. You're one of those women who are supposed to help one forget about life by rubbing one's nose in it." He turned round at the door.

"It's not she who's got me in her clutches, as you put it, it's I who fastened onto her."

"In that case, you should have told me a different story," she said gaily, shutting the door. He was shaking with rage as he went downstairs but he did not know against whom. He drove home at top speed, parked the car carelessly, and ran up the stairs. Behind the door, he could hear Nathalie's laugh and a man's voice. He took a deep breath. If it was the American, he would punch him in the nose; it would do both him and the American a great deal of good. Instead of using his key, he rang the bell, thinking how gentlemanly he was being. But Nathalie was still laughing as she opened the door to him.

"Guess who's here," she said.

Her brother was standing at the sitting-room door, smiling. Something in Gilles's expression made her ask:

"Why, who did you think it was?"

"I don't know," he said. "Hello, Pierre."

"Did you think it was Walter?"

"Walter?"

"The American, last night. I was just telling Pierre about him, and . . ."

She collapsed into an armchair, weeping with laughter. Her brother was beside her, laughing too, and the light-hearted atmosphere infected Gilles. They were like a pair of guileless children, charming to look at and somehow reassuring. Normal people—there were still some normal people left in the world. He fell into an armchair, exhausted but happy. He was at home, with people he belonged to, after an idiotic day caused by his own idiocy.

"How long have you been here?"

"Since this morning. I had a couple of free days and I wanted to see Nathalie. Her letters don't tell me enough."

Did she write to her brother often? Between museums? What in fact did she do with her days? When he came home, he told her all about his, and they would discuss politics like mad, talk about the paper and his friends, but never about her day-to-day activities. She had never really spoken to him about anything, anything that concerned her life, except her love for him. What could she have written to her brother? "I'm happy. . . . I'm bored. . . . Gilles is nice. . . . Gilles is not nice. . . ."? He glanced at Pierre, trying to read a reflection of her letters in his face, but he saw nothing. An affectionate curiosity, nothing more. No, she must be equally secretive with both of them. He thought of his visit to Gilda and was overcome with shame.

"But you haven't got a drink!" he said suddenly. "Nathalie's a deplorable hostess."

"Nathalie has always thought of herself as a guest wherever she is," said Pierre. "She can't help it."

He smiled. Nathalie hurried off to get some ice, leaving them alone for a minute or two.

"My sister seems happy," said Pierre.

He spoke calmly, but there was still the same menacing undertone in his voice as on that famous evening in Limoges. His "big brother" act still irritated Gilles.

"I certainly hope so," he said.

"I'd be delighted to be proved wrong," said the other peaceably. "At any rate, Limoges is dreary without her."

"I'm sorry to hear it," said Gilles. "But so would Paris be for me."

"That's the important thing. In fact, it's all I wanted to know."

"Hasn't she written to you?"

Pierre laughed.

"Nathalie never talks about her feelings. You should know that."

She returned carrying a tray rather awkwardly and Pierre jumped up to take it from her. Yes, she must have been loved and protected all her life, and she must often be alarmed by his outbursts—like those of a spoiled child. Between her and her brother there seemed to be a sort of reciprocity, a sense of mutual gratitude, the memory of countless kindnesses given and received, countless disinterested acts, and Gilles suddenly wished that he, too, had experienced this. All he could remember of his relationship with his sister was that it had been one-sided and rather silly, and as for women in general it was a history of scarcely veiled hostilities relieved by moments of happiness but always ending in victories that smacked of defeat, if not in defeat itself. He was dead-tired, he had drunk too much the night before, and he did not like himself.

"Why don't you two have dinner alone together?" he said. "You'll be more at your ease. I'll go to bed early. I'm whacked—I drank too much last night."

He was expecting them to protest, but Nathalie appeared delighted.

"Are you sure you don't mind? I haven't seen Pierre for such a long time. . . ."

"Do you mean it?" said Pierre.

"Poor Nathalie," thought Gilles, "you haven't seen anyone respectable for such a long time. Whom do you see, in fact? Nicholas, who's pretty far gone, Jean, who's jealous of you, your wretched school friend, who must be embittered, and the sad specimen whom you see before you and whom you're foolish enough to love." He shook his head.

"No, really. Go and have dinner without me. If I can't sleep, I'll have a hot drink with you when you get back."

When they had left, he switched on the television, switched it off again promptly, swallowed a piece of ham standing beside the refrigerator, and went to bed. He had a good detective story to read, a large bottle of mineral water at his elbow, cigarettes, and an excellent concert on the radio. Solitude certainly had its charms from time to time. In his heart of hearts he had always been a solitary, a good old lone wolf, and he was purring over this image of himself when he fell asleep with the light still on.

26

In due course, Nathalie decided to work. She announced to Gilles that she had found a very pleasant job in a travel agency, that she would be fairly well paid, and that this would help them with the monthly bills, which were sometimes a problem. He laughed at first, half-annoyed that she had managed to get herself fixed up without his help, half-amused at the idea of Nathalie behind a desk.

"What's come over you? Have you run out of museums?"

"I've got nothing to do all day," she said, "it gets me down."

"What did you do in Limoges?"

"There, I had my social work," she said calmly.

He burst out laughing. This woman was priceless.

"I know it sounds silly," she said, "but you know, I helped a great many people. . . ."

"All the same," he said, "you, as a lady bountiful . . . you spent all your afternoons in bed with me."

"That was in the summer," she said. "It's the winter that's the worst time for the poor."

He looked a her, dumfounded.

"Do you mean to say that if I had come to stay with my sister during the winter, I would never have gotten to know you?"

She hesitated, blushing.

"Yes," she said. "But that's not the point. This agency is extremely pleasant and the director is charming. He's a friend of Pierre's. Anyway, it's fun to plan journeys for people. I shall be sending them to Peru, or the West Indies, or New York."

"If you're only doing it for financial reasons, it's silly," he said. "We simply need to be a bit more careful."

Plainly it was he rather than she who squandered money, he never knew quite how. What with friends, bars, taxis, it simply ran through his fingers. And if Nathalie was able to get around, keep herself in clothes, it was thanks to the hundred thousand francs a month she received from an elderly aunt in the Limousin rather than to Gilles. He had not even finished paying for a beautiful antique brooch he had bought her for Christmas. No, it wasn't at all a bad idea, but for some reason it irritated Gilles.

"It's not for financial reasons," she said, "it's to keep me amused. But if you don't want me to, I'll say no."

"Do as you like," he said. "Speaking of travel, when does the florist get back?"

He was referring to Walter, who still persevered. He inundated Nathalie with roses—hence Gilles's nickname for him—and love letters. He had gone off on a trip and he sent a stream of sedate postcards from all over the place, with the equanimity of a man determined to wait for thirty years if necessary, which amused or exasperated Gilles depending on his mood. Nathalie herself was touched and, characteristically, made no secret of the fact, which was reassuring, of course, but prevented them from laughing about it together. Indeed, she maintained that there was nothing laughable about any passion, no matter what it was, and she even had long conversations on the subject with Garnier, to whom Gilles had introduced her one day, and who was still waiting for his friend to get out of prison. Garnier, as it turned out, was unloading more and more of his work on Gilles, and often, on arriving home, he found them talking earnestly by the fire. Nathalie certainly had peculiar tastes in people. Between the impotent Nicholas and the homosexual Garnier she bubbled over with gaiety and vivacity, whereas the company of Jean, who was equally intelligent, visibly oppressed her. "You don't understand," she said, when he took her to task about it, "there's something innocent about them that appeals to me," and he would shrug his shoulders, finding them rather boring but preferring them, as companions for her, to the American florist.

Nathalie duly started work and often, in the evenings, she would come to collect Gilles at the newspaper. The world was growing daily more insane, the editorial discussions longer and more violent, and Nathalie sometimes had to spend an hour or more waiting for Gilles in the bar below. Naturally she did not complain, but the thought of her waiting downstairs, inevitably rather bored, worried Gilles. In the end they decided they should go home separately and meet there. Thus it happened that one evening he never came home.

He had had an appalling day. Thomas, the egregious

Thomas, had overstepped the bounds of odiousness. Fairmont had called Gilles into his office to reprove him: apparently his articles were too "academic," lacking the excitement which appealed to "the reader." Gilles had never come across this famous reader he was always hearing about, this unknown soldier standing guard over the trivial, but if he had he would have given him a good hiding. According to Fairmont, "the reader" must be kept informed, objectively of course, but he must also be kept interested in, even excited about, any given subject.

"Don't you think the facts are exciting enough in themselves?" said Gilles sarcastically. "Wars all over the place . . ."

"There's no excitement for the reader unless he feels himself personally involved."

"But he *is* involved," said Gilles, exasperated. "Do you want me to give them the address of a recruiting office for Vietnam? Aren't the figures sufficiently eloquent?"

"You're the one who isn't eloquent."

Gilles had stamped out in a furious temper, condemned to completely rewrite his article at six o'clock in the evening. He had run into Garnier and asked him to let Nathalie know and, if possible, take her to dinner, a prospect at which Garnier seemed delighted, and he had sat alone in the office in front of his typewriter, more preoccupied with thinking up belated retorts to Fairmont than with the article. The paper was deserted and he walked up and down, sickened by his own prose. He went into Jean's office, opened the bottle of Scotch, and poured himself a generous glass, to no avail. He had had enough of this paper, he would never get anywhere, he would molder there for the rest of his life, being lectured by an increasingly senile Fairmont. He would age, Nathalie would turn into a provincial matron, they would probably marry and perhaps have children, they would buy a car and a cottage with TV. In fact they would be lucky if they got as far as that. It was a terrifying prospect. He, Gilles, capable of anything, ready to go anywhere, Gilles the Young, was in the process of wasting his life between a boss and a mistress who set themselves up as judges over him. Well, he had no wish to be judged, or to be pardoned, or even to be part of any system whatsoever, professional or emotional. He wanted to be free and independent, as he used to be. Like the gay young dog he had once been. He was drinking straight from the bottle now, savoring his rage. So he was supposed to stay in and correct his work like an obedient schoolboy in detention, was he? And he was supposed to go straight home to his loyal and faithful mistress, was he? Well, he would show them. He grabbed his raincoat and left, leaving all the lights on. The damned reader could pay the bill.

He awoke at midday in an unfamiliar, rather an only-too-familiar, bed, a bed in a brothel. A fat brunette was snoring at his side. He had a confused recollection of Montmartre night clubs, a brawl, a policeman's face; thank God he had chosen the Right Bank to go on his bender. He did not even have a headache, but he was dying of thirst. He got up and took a long swig of water from the enamel basin which so tastefully adorned the room. Then he went over to the window. It gave on a narrow, unfamiliar street. Inwardly he groaned. What could he have been up to? He shook the sleeping whore, who groaned and half opened her eyes, looking at him with a surprise which almost matched his own. She was quite hideous.

"Well, well," she said, "you had quite a load on."

"Where are we?"

"Near the boulevards. You owe me fifty smackers, ducky."

"What did I do?"

"Don't ask me. I picked you up at about half past five. I put you to bed and you were out like a light. Before that, I don't know."

He dressed at top speed. He put a bank note down on the bed and went to the door.

"Bye-bye, love," she said.

"Good-by."

The sun was high in the sky and he was in the Boulevard des Italiens. Nathalie, Nathalie, where was Nathalie at this time of day? Perhaps she was still at her office. No, she must be lunching next door, as usual. He took a taxi, his mind a blank. All he knew was that he must see her. But the agency was closed and there was no sign of her in the restaurant next door. He was frantic. He had kept the taxi and gave his own address on the off chance she was there. He opened the door noiselessly and froze on the threshold: Nathalie was there, sitting quietly in an armchair. He had the impression of reenacting a very old, very corny scene: the return of the wicked husband after a night's debauch.

"I got drunk," he said.

She said nothing. He saw the circles under her eyes. How old was she, exactly? She was wearing a little black dress and her new brooch; she must have sat there all night.

"I went to your office," he went on. "You weren't there . . . I . . . I'm desperately sorry, Nathalie. Have you been worried?"

He was talking a lot of nonsense; but really, what else was there to say? He was more relieved than anything else. He realized now that he had had one overriding fear in the taxi: that he would never find her again. But here she was. In fact she was almost smiling.

"Worried?" she said. "Why?"

165

He went towards her, and as he did so she rose and looked him in the face with a curious, almost puzzled expression. Then she slapped him violently, twice. After which she went into the kitchen.

"I'll make some coffee," she said in a calm voice.

Gilles stood stock-still. He felt nothing whatsoever, except that his cheeks stung; she had hit him infernally hard. Finally, he went toward the kitchen and propped himself against the door. She was watching the water boil with a show of great interest.

"Garnier stayed until three," she said with the same composure. "He telephoned the paper, then the Club. No sign of you. Then he telephoned Jean, who said you were in the habit of doing this sort of thing. He seemed to find it quite funny, which was comforting."

There was a searing irony in her voice.

"Since he wasn't aware that I was listening on the extension, he even told Garnier to advise me to get used to it. Because I would need to."

"Stop," said Gilles.

"I'm taking two minutes to describe a night that lasted twelve hours. That's hardly excessive."

"Anyone can get drunk once in a while."

"And anyone can telephone and say, 'I'm getting drunk, don't wait up.' But I imagine that would have spoiled your pleasure."

"She's right," thought Gilles. "It was the idea of my guilt which spurred me on last night."

"Here's some coffee," she said. "Now you've had everything you wanted: a night on the town, a row with your mistress, a slap in the face, a cup of coffee. Yes? Then I'll be off to my office." She picked up her coat and went out. He stood for a moment stunned, then drank his coffee and opened the newspaper. But he did not read it. It was neither jealousy nor anger that he had aroused in her. It was first of all anxiety, then contempt. The telephone rang and he leaped to answer it. Perhaps she was sorry for having been so harsh.

"Well, old boy," said Jean's voice, "I gather you're up to your old tricks again."

"Yes," said Gilles.

"Are you alone?"

"Yes."

Jean's voice was cheerful, conspiratorial. But something in Gilles hesitated to succumb to his voice and what it implied.

"How did the homecoming go? Badly?"

"A slap in the face," said Gilles, and as Jean began to laugh, he realized that he had in fact succumbed.

27

He was aware now that something between them had cracked. He did not know precisely what—perhaps it was simply that he had been deprived of a jealous scene; perhaps, without realizing it, he needed her to do something shabby or despicable which would put them once more on an equal footing. Could it have been that one night of drunkenness—trivial, in all conscience, and excusable—which had caused a displacement of their two images, putting Nathalie's above his, or was it the inevitable penalty for six months of living together? Was she better than he? Can one be "better" than the other in a love relationship, the one relationship in which all moral values are supplanted by affective ones? Whatever the reason, she laughed less than before, she was getting thinner, and there was something aggressive, something deliberately violent, in their purely physical relation, as though each wanted at the same time to satiate and subjugate the other, as though the other's pleasure was no longer the wonderful gift they had up to now considered it, but was merely a test of their love. But what availed these cries, these moans, these spasms? What availed these poor bodies, however perfectly united, after certain looks from Nathalie and in the absence of certain looks from Gilles? They proved nothing: they were indispensable but insufficient, they came together in pleasure again and again, but in vain. Gilles had never been so much in love with anyone, physically, and felt so little joy in being so.

There came a day when she had to go to Limoges. Her aunt Mathilde, the source of the monthly stipend, was dying and had summoned her. She was to stay with her brother, and return as soon as possible. Gilles drove her to the station, to Austerlitz, the station which had seen his own unhappy departure eight months before, his carefree return, his second departure as a lover, his final return as a committed man. He did not know which he liked best of the travelers he had been. Ah, yes, it was the lover of last May, conscious of his love, not expecting to be met, who had watched the Loire, the suburbs, the clouds, the night roll by like so many dazzling surprises before the crowning surprise of Nathalie, a fugitive from her dinner party, there on the platform, rushing toward him. He loved the story of their romance, even if, at times, he did not love their life together. He had even come to feel an affection for that gaunt, sad, miserable young man he had so hated being, and he loved that passionate, reckless, immoderate, and extremely respectable woman who had fallen in love with him. He thought of the meadows of the Limousin, and the warm grass, and the riverbed. He remembered the touch of Nathalie's hand on his neck, and the lugubrious bed in which they had first made love, and the look the innkeeper had given them, and the stuffy attic room, and Florent's eggnogs. . . . What were they doing now, prowling around this station like two lost animals, searching for something to say to each other, regulating their watches, buying stupid magazines? What had happened? He glanced at Nathalie's clean-cut profile, he looked back over the past three months in Paris, and he no longer knew what to think. He did not want her to leave, but if, for some extraordinary reason, the train were held up near Orléans, say, and she were obliged to come back to the flat with him, he would have been furious. He was due to dine with Jean and some other friends, nothing special, nothing at any rate as important to him as this woman was, and yet he longed for her to go away, for her train to leave early. He was mad: he was possessed by this wretched madman who hankered after a futile independence.

He gave her a long kiss, and watched her walk away down the passage. Before him lay the city, huge and furrowed like a closeup of the moon, an arid, brightly lit city, a city at his disposal. Yes, Nathalie was right when she said that he was perfectly adapted to his time.

"It's everything that you most like," she had said. "You claim to detest the inherent stupidity of this century, its lies and its violence. Yet you take to it like a duck to water. You're only happy when you're in the thick of it, swimming against the current, of course, but with what skill! You may switch off the television, turn off the radio, but how you enjoy doing it! It distinguishes you."

"What about you?" he said, "which century would you have liked?"

"I should have liked to be able to admire," she said.

Admire . . . A woman ought not to say such things. A woman ought to be content to admire the man she lived with, not fill her head with these puerile hankerings.

He was a little late in joining the others, and received a discreetly triumphal welcome; very discreetly triumphal, to be sure, but the sort of welcome reserved for a man restored to liberty. "There's Gilles!" someone cried, and they all laughed as he bowed with his hand on his heart. Of course, they would never say "There's Gilles and Nathalie" in the same tone. But he couldn't blame them: pleasure lovers are, above all, creatures of habit, and he had been playing lone wolf often accompanied by a woman, but always a woman who could be left at a table or with a friend, like Eloise, for example, who knew everybody and whom he would cheerfully abandon, knowing that the first fellow to turn up would come and sit at her table, or else some girl friend would. Only, he had Nathalie in his life nowadays, Nathalie, who must at this moment be passing through Orléans.

He spent a quiet evening, drank little, and went home alone at about half past twelve. He had Pierre's telephone number and he rang up as soon as he got in. Nathalie answered at once and he told her tenderly that he was in their flat, listening to some Mozart, and that the bed seemed much too big without her. He embroidered on this a little, dazzled by his own rectitude.

"The train journey was endless," said Nathalie, "I don't like that trip. Are you all right?"

Her voice sounded distant, the line was bad, he had to search for words. If he had been up to no good, he would certainly have had a great deal more to say to her. Lying stimulates one's imagination and ingenuity.

"I'm going to bed now," he said briskly, "I've got a lot of work ahead of me tomorrow. I think about you all the time."

"Me too. Sleep well, darling."

She hung up. They might have been married for ten

years. He took off his tie with a yawn and looked at himself in the mirror. He would stretch himself out on this bed, just so, listen to a good concert (easy enough at that hour—he had only been anticipating when he mentioned Mozart to Nathalie), just so, and he would sleep like a child, wake up in excellent form tomorrow, work like a demon, just so, and await the return of his beloved. But his reflection stared back at him; he saw this stranger smiling, realized that he himself was smiling. He picked up his jacket and went out, banging the door.

"We were just saying . . ."

He was in the Club, Jean was laughing, he felt aglow in the company of his friends, friends who might be true or false, but were at any rate gay, ready for anything, friends whom he had after all seriously neglected for the sake of a woman. That was not very nice of him: such people's equilibrium was easily upset, one couldn't play truant from the evening class for too long, it demoralized them. He leaned over to Jean:

"I really meant to go home to bed, and then suddenly, when I got to the flat, I couldn't sleep. I don't like sleeping alone."

"That should be easy to put right," said Jean's girl friend.

She was very vulgar this evening, he thought. He had always found her insignificant, but never vulgar. Jean had not winced, however, and he thought that he must be imagining things. That it was Nathalie who had put these notions of good or bad taste into his head, and that it was really rather boring.

"There's always Catherine," he said. She was a magnificent looking blonde who had always allowed him to think that she was attracted to him and she happened to be passing their table at that moment.

"I wouldn't recommend her," said Jean. "She gossips like a magpie, and Nathalie would hear about it."

No question about it, Jean was talking to him as though he were a runaway schoolboy. But Gilles could not decide whether Jean wished to spare Nathalie's feelings or to underline his dependence on her.

"I'm a big boy now," he said vaguely. "Anyway, it would take more than a Catherine to upset things between Nathalie and me."

"I wouldn't be so sure," said Jean quietly. "She's got quite a temper, your Nathalie."

He smiled with an air of compassion. Gilles threw him an inquiring glance from which, as with all inquiring glances, he learned nothing. It was only the casual glance which informed. No doubt about it, he was in a bad mood. When Nathalie was there, he felt trapped, when she wasn't there, it was almost worse. Wasn't that what was called "ruining" someone's life? In all the looks which he intercepted, all the remarks which were made to him, he saw himself as "the chap who's in love with a woman and who's on his own for the evening" or "the chap whose mistress has him on a leash and who's breaking loose." (Neither of which was his case.) If he just sat where he was, he would look miserable. If he made a pass at Catherine, here in the Club, he would humiliate Nathalie, and himself. He sighed, and asked for the bill. All he had done was to waste an hour.

28

He had done more than waste an hour. As he realized next morning when he telephoned Nathalie on waking up.

"I forgot to tell you last night that your blue suit was ready at the cleaners," she said. "I called back, but there was no answer."

Naturally not, since he had gone out within a minute of making his dutiful call to her. Gone out for nothing, moreover, but how was she to believe that, now? Truth and falsehood were in league against him. Yet he had really meant to stay in at that particular moment.

"I assumed you would go and see your friends," said Nathalie's voice, "but why all that song and dance? Am I such an ogress? Why talk of being at home and the bed being too big and the music? Why, Gilles?"

"I *wanted* to stay in," he said, "when I called you. Then I suddenly decided to go out."

"A minute later?"

It rang false, the truth rang hopelessly false, there was nothing he could do about it. Nevertheless he went on.

"I had a drink with Jean at the Club and I was home again within an hour."

("And not only, because of you, did I do nothing about that delicious Catherine, not only did I behave like an angel, but I've made you unhappy and you think I'm lying." He was angry, and yet he sympathized with her: he was innocent, and yet convicted of lying.)

"It's not what you do or don't do," said Nathalie. "It's what you say, what you feel obliged to say."

He sighed, lit a cigarette, and ran his fingers through his hair.

"I'll explain when I see you," he said. "How's your aunt?"

"Very ill. In fact, she's sure to die in a day or two. I'm going over there in a minute, with Pierre."

Of course, there was Pierre, who must have been there last night when his sister answered the telephone, her voice tender, and then, exclaiming "Oh, goodness, the cleaners!" had called back, and getting no reply, had turned to him with an unnaturally calm expression. One often does more harm to people through their nearest and dearest than directly. For then, out of pride, they have to gloss things over, think up excuses, waste their energy, apparently forgetting all about the telephone near at hand. Alone, Nathalie might well have called him every half hour, and she would have reached him at the second try. God, how absurd life was!

"Nathalie," he said, "I love you."

"So do I," she said, but there was no trace of gaiety in her voice, only a resigned acceptance.

She hung up. In a week's time, he would explain everything to her; he would hold her in his arms, he would feel her warm, live, receptive body against his, instead of that blank, stony face, instead of those bleak, meaningless phrases which they had to make do with on the telephone. As for the others (he did not know precisely who "the others" were, imagining a huge menacing swarm of Parisians buzzing round him), they too would see. Or rather, not see. Not see *him,* for a week, first of all, then not see *them,* at all, once she was back. They would either stay at home or they would go to the theater, because she liked the theater, or to a concert, because he liked music. Of course what he really preferred was listening to a good record lying sprawled on the carpet, but he would do what had to be done. Comforted by this idea, he got up singing, left early for the paper, and did a good day's work. He was appalled to find himself in the Club at three o'clock the next morning, arguing with an English journalist about segregation in the States.

She arrived ten days later, at eleven o'clock in the evening, at their beloved Austerlitz station. She approached in the middle of a merry throng of provincial ladies, and she was dressed as they were, her skirt a little too long, a silk scarf round her head, carrying her little suitcase. Apart from her bearing and her beauty, there was nothing to distinguish her from the others. He had lived with women whose lackeys had carried pet dogs like bouquets of flowers, and he had found it tiresome at the time. But now, in this gray and gloomy station (it was raining), he would have liked to see his mistress arrive in a splash of color, like some baroque creature. He took her in his arms and kissed her. She had rings under her eyes and she was in mourning—of course, what a fool he was!

"Ah, it's you," she said, clinging to him, motionless. People were staring at them and he felt somehow ashamed: after all, they weren't children, making an exhibition of themselves in a railway station. He tried to make a joke of it.

"Why, who did you think it was?"

"You," she said. "Just you."

She had raised her eyes to his and he gazed at her intently. Her features looked slightly swollen, he thought, and she was badly made-up. He did not find his scrutiny any more out of the ordinary than his presence there. He had come to the station to collect his mistress, his wife to all intents and purposes, and he was looking at her as all old lovers look at each other. He took her arm.

"I've bought some cold chicken, we'll eat at home. Did you leave straight after the funeral?"

"Yes, of course. As you can imagine, Limoges wasn't particularly pleasant."

"Did decent folk throw stones at you?"

"Oh, no," she said, "they know the flesh is weak. They read the newspapers these days."

She glanced abstractedly at the mess which he had managed to make in the two hours he had spent in the flat before leaving for the station, then went to the bathroom to redo her face while he cut up the chicken, swearing profusely. After coffee, they went into the sitting room and he carefully put on the new Haydn record he had just bought.

"Well," she said, "what's been happening in Paris?"

She spoke listlessly, her eyes closed, in a tone that seemed to suggest that nothing could really happen in Paris.

"Not much," he said. "Have you read the papers?"

"And what about you?"

Still the same voice. He smiled.

"Nothing much either. I've been working hard. And drinking a bit too much, perhaps, in your absence, and I've bought this record."

He omitted to add that he had finally, when very drunk, gone home with the lovely Catherine, and it had been a total fiasco. At least she would keep quiet for once. She had all the more reason to conceal Gilles's sudden impotence, since he now knew all her little ways. He held out his hand to Nathalie, who took it.

"And what about you? Did you see François?"

"Yes," she said, "of course. He came to see me at Pierre's."

"Why?"

"He wanted me to go back to him. I think he's bored."

"The provinces have changed," said Gilles.

He was a little annoyed, without knowing why. Men were always wanting to take this woman away from him; not imagining for one moment that she loved him, that she could love him. Clearly he was an accident in her life.

"And what did you say to him?"

"I said no. That I loved you. That I was very sorry. Pierre wanted me to stay, too."

A kind of anger welled up inside Gilles. True, he had fooled around a bit during the past ten days, played the gay young bachelor. But what had it amounted to? Two hours with a depraved little bitch and night after night talking his head off to people whose minds were sodden with drink or conformism. During this time, she had been confronting real men, known men, abruptly stripped of their pride, she had been living, she had been playing Anna Karenina in reverse. She had been suffering remorse, regrets even, in a word, she had been feeling.

"I don't even know why I'm telling you all this," she said. "I'm so tired. So you're pleased with your work?"

Was she about to give him a good mark? He could not understand this jealousy of his, this rage. After all, she had come back to him. She had left everything for him. She was there. What was he afraid of?

"I saw your sister and Florent, too—at the funeral. She complained about not having heard from you. You should have written to them."

"I'll do it tomorrow," he said.

He made an effort to control his voice, his trembling hands. He even managed a smile.

"You ought to go to bed," he said. "You're worn out. I'll join you."

Left alone, he took a gulp of whiskey straight from the bottle, burning his throat. Presently he would go and make love to this perfect companion, this perfect mistress, this perfect everything. Life was very well ordered really. He would even be able to say to her presently "I've missed you, you know," without lying. Nevertheless he was shivering.

29

She had indeed burned her bridges, severed all links with her past, her childhood, her friends. Her brother had tormented her with advice and entreaties, and her husband had presented her with an ultimatum: "Come back now or leave for good." She confessed all this to Gilles in brief snatches in the dark, and he was grateful for the dark which hid her tears from him. Clearly no one in the Limousin had any confidence in Gilles, including his own sister, Odile, who had taken Nathalie aside in a sudden burst of boldness and asked if she was happy, as though that were the last thing to be expected. "There's nothing left for me there," Nathalie told him, and he often wondered whether they, the solid landowners, had not been right. Meanwhile the days went by, April was turning the trees green once more, and they lived as best they could. One morning, Gilles arrived at the paper in a triumphant mood. He had written an excellent article on

Greece the day before, which had fascinated Nathalie when he read it to her, and he was bursting with self-confidence. Sure enough, Fairmont thought it excellent, as did Jean, and even Garnier, who had been avoiding him somewhat since his famous night out, congratulated him. The article was terse, vehement, and to the point, the sort of article they ought to have at least once a week, Fairmont said. Gilles was delighted, and as they were putting the paper to bed that morning, he invited Jean to lunch with him. They talked politics throughout the meal and then, feeling slothful, decided to go to the cinema. They walked up and down the Champs Elysées without finding a film which the other had not already seen.

"I won't ask you back home," said Jean. "It's Marthe's day for having friends round. I can't let you in for that."

"Let's go to my place," said Gilles. "Nathalie won't be back until half past six. But in any case I'd like to talk to you a bit more about the Greek business."

He was in a keen, analytical frame of mind and was delighted to have a chance to exercise his wits for another hour or two on Jean, whom he knew to be a good listener and debater. He opened the door of his flat, invited Jean to sit down, and poured him a glass of Calvados.

"It's a long time since I've been here," said Jean as he sat down.

There was no reproach in his voice, but Gilles thought how true it was. His flat had been full of people before, sprawled all over the place. Before . . . before Nathalie. He gave a slight grimace.

"You know . . ."

"I know, I know, old boy," said Jean. "A passion is a passion. And it's the best thing that could have happend to you. Especially with someone like Nathalie."

He seemed absolutely sincere.

"Yes and no," said Gilles, and he leaned forward. Once more he felt analytical, subtle, Proustian. One never feels disloyal when one feels intelligent.

"You see, when I first met her, I was . . . well, you remember . . . I felt flayed alive. God knows why, but I did. She feather-bedded me, kept me warm, brought me back to life. Truly. But now . . ."

"Now what?"

"Now it's as though I'm being smothered, I'm suffocating. Everything I used to love about her, everything that buoyed me up, her positiveness, her directness, her complete integrity . . . it's all working against her."

"Because you're weak and unstable," said Jean affectionately.

"If you like. Perhaps I'm nothing but a worthless bastard. But there are times when . . . when . . . I'd give anything not to be judged by her. And to be on my own, as I used to be."

He should have added, in the interest of accuracy, that he could not imagine life without her. But in the elation of having written his article, the aura of general approbation, and Jean's sympathetic interest, he let it go.

"Perhaps you could explain things to her," said Jean.

But he broke off abruptly. Gilles turned round and saw Nathalie standing in the doorway that led to the bedroom. She looked calm, but perhaps her eyes were brighter than usual. Had the door been closed when they came in?

"Good afternoon," said Jean.

He had stood up. He too was rather pale.

"Are you talking shop?" said Nathalie. "The agency was

closed this afternoon so I had the chance to sleep for a while."

"I . . . you were sleeping?" said Gilles in desperation.

"I've just waked up. I've got some shopping to do, so I'll leave you."

"Do stay," said Gilles quickly, "please stay. I was just talking to Jean about that article—the one I read to you yesterday."

"Wasn't it good?" she said to Jean. "No, really, I must go out."

She smiled at them and left. They sat down again slowly.

"Christ almighty!" swore Gilles. "Christ! Do you think? . . ."

"No, I don't think so," said Jean. "I seem to remember that the door was shut. Anyway, you didn't say anything very serious. You merely said that there were moments when you felt a bit fed up. Every woman knows that."

Oh, but it *was* serious. In fact is was horribly serious.

"But don't you see," he shouted. "For me to be talking about my relations with her like that, and with you of all people . . ."

"What do you mean, me of all people? What have I done?"

"Nothing," said Gilles, "nothing. This is no time to get annoyed."

"Don't worry," said Jean soothingly. "Let's just finish the Calvados and wait. There'll be a bit of a row tonight, at the worst. But you're used to that."

"No," said Gilles pensively. "No, I'm not used to it."

Time flew, stood still. He scarcely heard what Jean was saying: he was listening for footsteps on the staircase. She had been gone for an hour, an hour and a half—she who loathed shopping. It simply wasn't credible. He telephoned

Garnier hoping for news, but he hadn't seen Nathalie. At five o'clock it suddenly struck him that she was going to take the train back home. He abandoned Jean, rushed to the station, and searched up and down the train, without finding her. No, there hadn't been an earlier train. No, there were no planes to Limoges that day. At six o'clock the train left without him, without her. She had not come. He drove back on his tracks, almost sobbing with rage in the traffic jams. . . . Perhaps she was back at the flat? Perhaps she had overheard nothing? It was nearly seven o'clock when he opened the door. The flat was empty, except for a note from Jean.

"Don't worry too much. Come and dine with us, if you feel like it."

The man must be mad! There was only one thing to do: wait, the thing he detested most in the world. Perhaps she was with her old schoolfriend. He rushed to the telephone. But she was not there. It was unbearable. When she came back he would give her a good slap in the face. She had been absolutely right that morning, after his night out. But it wasn't like Nathalie to worry people to death like this, deliberately. She had some consideration for other people. He sat down in an armchair, but did not even attempt to read a newspaper. There was a great resounding emptiness in his head. At midnight, the telephone rang.

The doctor was a small, red-haired man, with muscular hands covered with hairs. It was odd how much hair red-haired people had on their hands. He looked at Gilles with that impersonal expression, neither accusing nor sympathetic, which he had often seen in hospitals. Nathalie had been found at half past eleven. She had taken a room in a hotel at exactly four o'clock, said she was tired, asked to be called the following day at noon, and swallowed the necessary quantity of gardenol. The person in the room next door had come back at about eleven and had heard her gasping for breath. She had left a note for Gilles and they had telephoned him as soon as they had given her emergency treatment. There was not much hope: the body had rebelled, of course, at the last moment; the body had complained but the heart would not hold out.

"Can I see her?" asked Gilles.

He could hardly stand. The whole thing was nothing but a stupid nightmare. The doctor shrugged his shoulders.

"If you wish . . ."

She was surrounded by tubes, half-naked, her face distorted by something he could not guess at. He watched the blue vein beating in her neck, remembered how furiously it throbbed in the act of love, and felt oddly indignant. She couldn't have done this to him, taken away from him forever that beautiful living body so attuned to his, she couldn't have tried to escape from him. Locks of Nathalie's hair were stuck to her forehead with sweat, and her hands stirred on the sheets. There was a nurse standing beside her bed who glanced inquiringly at the door.

"The heart's failing," she said.

"Off you go, old man, I'll be with you in a moment," said the doctor. "You're not needed here."

Gilles left the room and leaned against the wall outside. There was a window at the end of the corridor and it was still night, black night over this heartless city. He put his hand in his pocket, felt a piece of paper, and drew it out mechanically. It was Nathalie's letter. He opened it and took a moment or two to grasp what he read.

"It's not your fault, my darling. I was always a bit too intense and I have never loved anyone but you." She had signed it with a big "N," slightly askew. He put the letter back in his pocket. Where could he have put his cigarettes? And Nathalie, next door, where had he put Nathalie? The doctor came out of the room. He really was horribly red-haired.

"It's all over, old man," he said. "Too late. I'm sorry. Do you want to see her?"

But Gilles had already fled, was running blindly toward the other end of the corridor, could not bear to have this redhead see his tears. Now he was plunging down the stairs in this nameless hospital; he hardly heard the doctor's voice shouting after him. On the bottom step, he paused, his heart beating.

"What about filling out these forms?" the voice was saying from up there, a long way away, "what about these forms? She had only you?"

He hesitated an instant, before answering what he knew was the truth.

"Yes."